·T·H· Fear Place

BOOKS BY PHYLLIS REYNOLDS NAYLOR

THE WITCH TRILOGY
Witch's Sister
Witch Water
The Witch Herself

Walking through the Dark

AUTOBIOGRAPHY
How I Came to Be a Writer

How Lazy Can You Get?
Eddie, Incorporated

THE YORK TRILOGY
Shadows on the Wall
Faces in the Water
Footprints at the Window

All Because I'm Older

The Boy with the Helium Head
A String of Chances
The Solomon System
Night Cry
Old Sadie and the Christmas Bear
The Dark of the Tunnel

T·H·E
Fear Place

PHYLLIS REYNOLDS NAYLOR

ALADDIN PAPERBACKS

With special thanks to Douglas Caldwell and Jim Wilson of the National Park Service, Rocky Mountain National Park, for their help and cooperation in my research

First Aladdin Paperbacks edition March 1996
Copyright © 1994 by Phyllis Reynolds Naylor

Aladdin Paperbacks
An imprint of Simon & Schuster
Children's Publishing Division
1230 Avenue of the Americas
New York, NY 10020

Also available in an Atheneum Books for Young Readers edition
Designed by Sarah González Lauck
The text of this book was set in Perpetua.
Printed and bound in the United States of America
15 14 13 12 11 10 9 8

The Library of Congress has cataloged the hardcover edition as follows:
Naylor, Phyllis Reynolds.
The Fear Place / Phyllis Reynolds Naylor.—1st ed.   p.   cm.
Summary: When he and his older brother Gordon are left camping alone in the Rocky Mountains, twelve-year-old Doug faces his fear of heights and his feelings about Gordon—with the help of a cougar.
ISBN 0-689-31866-9
[1. Brothers—Fiction. 2. Fear—Fiction. 3. Pumas—Fiction.
4. Camping—Fiction.] I. Title.
PZ7.N24Fe 1994   [Fic]—dc20   93-38891
ISBN 0-689-80442-3 (Aladdin pbk.)

To Dan Metcalfe, whom I met on the train

CHAPTER 1

IT WAS WHEN GORDON PUSHED PAST HIM UP THE STEPS TO THE PLANE, that the anger surfaced again. He was trying to get the window seat, Doug was sure of it. In their parents' eyes, he knew, it was something so small that it wasn't even worth talking about. A nothing, compared to the stress of recent months.

But to Doug, it was just one more insult to add to the mountain of grievances that had been growing over the past few years— longer than that, maybe—so long he couldn't even remember. Maybe that's how it was with brothers.

"Gordie!" he hissed as they edged by the smiling flight attendant at the top.

His brother didn't even turn around.

"Gordie!" Doug hissed again. "I get the window seat. Mom *said*!"

At row seventeen, Gordon swung himself in next to the window.

"Move!" Doug insisted. "You had it last time."

"So what? You've had it twice in a row before."

"I never did!"

A large bag bumped against his leg as a man tried to get past.

"Excuse me," the man said.

"Doug, will you please find one of the other seats?" said Mom, coming up behind him. "Take 20C."

"Mom, Gordon's got . . ."

"Could I get by, please?" A heavyset woman pushed past Mother and glared at Doug.

"For heaven's sake, Doug, take another seat!" Every inch of Mother's face showed strain and exasperation. "I don't *care* who sits where. Just *sit*!"

Furious, Doug reached over and socked Gordon's arm, then stomped on down the aisle and slid into 20C next to a kid who was playing Game Boy and chewing gum.

The boy glanced over. "Hi. What's your name?" he asked. Right off the bat. Just like that.

Doug didn't feel like talking to anyone, but he did: "Doug Grillo. What's yours?"

"Grillo? What kind of name is that?" the boy asked. And then, without waiting for an answer, "Mine's Ronnie Beck."

"Yeah? What kind of name is that?" Doug retorted. He was steamed.

The boy studied him, then shrugged. "Don't have a cow," he said.

This is going to be the lousiest trip I've ever taken. Doug leaned back in the seat and watched his father put his carry-on bag in the overhead compartment. This is what happens when you're late getting to the airport: All the good seats are gone. When the taxi had come that morning, Gordon had to go to the bathroom at the last minute, and then they were two miles from home when Mom realized she'd forgotten the tickets. With Uncle Lloyd so sick up in Boston, though, she'd had a lot on her mind lately. Doug could understand that.

They were scattered like plants in the desert—Doug halfway back with this Nintendo nerd; Gordon three rows up on the other side by the window; Mom beside Gordon; and Dad two rows up from them, on the aisle.

The really weird thing was that Doug didn't even like the window seat. He just wanted a choice. Just wanted things fifty-fifty. It never seemed like that. It was more like Doug, forty; Gordon, sixty; Doug, twenty; Gordon, eighty.

Why couldn't his parents see that? Why couldn't they understand that it wasn't an argument about window seats or the last piece of chocolate cake or who got the new bike and who got the used one? It was an argument about fairness. It was . . .

"I hate to fly," said Ronnie Beck, rubbing the palm of one hand on his jeans. "That's why I bring a game—so I won't notice when the plane takes off."

"Why do you fly, then?"

The kid shrugged again. "You do what you have to do."

"You alone?"

"Yeah. My parents split. I'm meeting Dad in Denver."

Ahead three rows, Doug saw his mother's blond head tilt backward, rest for a moment against the seat, then turn. She smiled at him, wanting to retie the family bonds, to "make nice." He stared straight ahead. Mother turned back again.

"That your mom?" Ronnie Beck didn't miss a thing.

"Yeah."

"Where's your dad?"

As if on cue, Dad stood up again and turned around to check on the family. Dark thick hair, black mustache, dusky skin . . .

"Him?" said Ronnie.

Doug nodded.

"Grillo's Spanish, huh?"

"Clever kid."

"My dad's one part English, one part Scotch, and two parts German."

Maybe he wasn't obnoxious, just talky. Nosy and talky.

"Mine escaped from Cuba." The words fell out of Doug's mouth unintended.

Ronnie Beck turned in his seat and stared at him. "Was he a prisoner or something?"

"*No*, he wasn't a prisoner! He didn't like living under Castro. Jeez, don't you know anything?"

"I don't know Castro," Ronnie said.

Doug sighed and leaned back in his seat. "How come you don't like to fly?"

"Why do you think? 'Cause I don't want to die."

"You fly a lot?"

"Denver and back every summer."

"Well, you haven't died yet. You probably do a lot more dangerous things than flying and never even think about it. You have a bike?"

"Yeah."

"Well, more people die on bikes, I'll bet, than in plane crashes."

"Yeah. It doesn't help, though."

Doug understood. He wasn't all that fond of planes himself, and felt that familiar tightness in his chest during takeoffs and landings. But planes were enclosed; a seat belt held him fast. It was a different place that turned his lungs to ice—a high place, a rocky place, a narrow crumbling path six hundred feet above a canyon: the Fear Place.

2

THE SUN SHINING ON THE WING REFLECTED INTO DOUG'S EYES. IF HE was over by the window he could close the shade, but the man sitting next to Ronnie Beck was taking pictures.

When the man leaned back a little, Doug could see a bed of clouds beyond, as though one could open the window and step right out on to cream puffs. He liked that, not being able to see below. You usually couldn't.

Up ahead, Gordon peered over the back of his seat and gave Doug that "I won" grin, then slid down again.

The rush of anger returned. Man, Doug hated him. Mom said that "hate" was too strong a word to use for passing emotions, to save it for the really big things, like what the Nazis did to the Jews. She didn't realize that how Doug felt about his older brother wasn't passing. It was 95 percent of the time. Well, 85, maybe.

If the plane crashed right now, Doug was thinking, and Mom and Dad escaped, would he stop to rescue Gordon or just go on? Doug closed his eyes and tried to play it out. He couldn't imagine either saving him or leaving him behind.

He leaned forward to put his boarding pass in his hip pocket and realized he was holding his father's. *Antonio Grillo* it said on the stub. He wondered who in the family was holding his. Gordon, maybe. He smiled just a little. That would be justice, all right. If Gordon had to be him all the way to Denver.

Doug looked more like their mother than Gordon did—light hair, dark eyes, thin lips rather than the full mouth of Gordon's and Dad's. But he had his dad's physique—short and muscular. Strong as an ox, Mother said. Doug was about twenty pounds heavier than Gordon, even though he was younger. It was Gordon who had a lean torso like Mom's. When the boys were on camp-outs together, Doug could carry a lot more weight than Gordon could. He'd even carried Gordie once in a four-man race where you had to run with your partner on your shoulders.

The flight attendant was moving down the aisle with a cart. The man by the window lowered his tray table, so Doug and Ronnie lowered theirs. Flip, flip, flip—the flight attendant slung plastic plates on each tray table as though she were dealing cards. Doug figured she flew out of Vegas.

"I don't want any," he said, glancing down at the rubbery omelette, the dry-looking roll, the watery fruit juice, and the orange slice beside a single strawberry. Actually, he wouldn't mind the orange slice and strawberry.

The flight attendant gave him a tolerant smile and was about to remove the plate when Ronnie said, "I'll eat it."

"Fine," the flight attendant said, and left it there on Doug's tray.

Doug bet that was against the rules. He bet if he had been the man by the window, she would have removed the plate; at *least* put the extra plate on Ronnie's tray. Kids got treated the worst. Especially younger kids. Doug was twelve, only eighteen months younger than Gordon, and he still got the short end of the stick.

"You have any brothers or sisters?" he asked the boy beside him.

Ronnie chewed hard on the roll, then swallowed—a large gulp, that made him tuck his chin under. "Nope."

"Lucky."

"Why?"

"See that guy up there, over by the window?" Doug said, pointing to the seat where a mop of hair, dark like his father's, emerged from time to time. "That's my brother."

"How come you don't like him?"

"Did I say I didn't?" Ronnie was really beginning to get on his nerves.

"Well, do you?"

"Not much."

"Why not?"

"Because he knows a million ways to make me mad."

"Why does he do it?"

That stumped Doug for a moment. The "why" of it never crossed his mind. He wasn't sure there even was a why. It just was. The way Gordie was.

"I don't know." Doug waited a moment and then reached for the orange slice and strawberry. "I guess I'll just eat these."

Ronnie's hand shot out like lightning. "You said you didn't want any breakfast, so I get these, too."

Jeez, what an obnoxious kid! "Forget it."

"If you still want them, though, I'll make a deal."

Doug stared at him. "They were mine in the first place."

"But not anymore; you gave them to me. I'll sell them back to you for a quarter."

"Go soak your head."

"A dime then."

"Look, will you forget it? Just clam up and eat."

"Your choice," said Ronnie, and wolfed the fruit down.

For a long time the two boys sat side- by side not saying anything, just listening to the quiet hum of the plane. Ronnie even picked up his game again, and then, without warning, asked another question. "How did he get out of Cuba?"

"On a raft," Doug told him.

"Wow! When?"

"Before I was born."

"Oh." Ronnie Beck went back to his Game Boy.

The plane got into Denver around eleven, Mountain time, and Doug was starved for lunch, but of course the flight attendant wasn't serving any.

He had noticed the way Ronnie clutched the arms of the seat as the plane made its landing. For a brief moment Doug thought of saying something friendly to help him through it, but then he remembered the orange slice and strawberry, and didn't.

As he was getting his bag down, though, he said, "Well, have a good time with your dad."

"Yeah." Ronnie wrinkled up his nose. "He likes sports, I like this." He held up the Game Boy before shoving it into his flight bag. "Maybe I'll see you on the plane back to Virginia."

"Maybe. So long."

"Bye," said Ronnie.

Mother was getting something out of her bag, so Doug moved on up the aisle beside his dad.

"Pretty sky out there, what we could see of it, huh?" his father said.

Doug nodded.

"Want a candy bar? I picked one up in the airport and forgot to eat it." Dad reached into his jacket pocket and pulled out a Mounds bar, the big kind, in two fat sections.

"Sure." Doug smiled and slipped it in his own pocket.

They had a long wait at the baggage pickup for their gear. When it came, Doug watched Ronnie Beck go off with a big man who was one part English, one part Scotch, and two parts German. The man had an arm around Ronnie's shoulder, but Ronnie was carrying his flight bag between them, and it kept bumping against his dad's leg.

There was another wait at the car rental desk, and finally, loaded with backpacks and bags, the family moved across the lot to a Ford Bronco. Before Doug had a chance to think, Gordon sprinted over to the passenger side and climbed in front beside his father.

Doug and Mother got in back.

"Well," she said, reaching over and giving him a quick pat on the knee. "Our fifth time here!"

Dad turned the key in the ignition. Gordon was already fiddling with knobs and dials.

"Enjoy it, guys, because our grant's up this year. We'll be winding up the research." Dad smiled at Doug in the rearview mirror. And then, to Gordon, "I might even let you do some driving on a back road somewhere. Give you a little experience, huh?"

Gordon turned and flashed Doug his usual triumphant grin. Doug didn't even bat an eye. He was holding a huge Mounds bar right in front of him, slowly pulling off the wrapper. And then, when Gordie did a double take, he closed his lips around it and savored the first bite.

CHAPTER 3

THEY DROVE TO ESTES PARK AND SPENT THE REST OF THE DAY MAK-ing purchases; batteries, the powdered and dehydrated foods they'd be eating for the next three weeks, fuel for the stove. . . . The Grillos always stayed at a motel the first night, and set out for the trailhead by car the next morning.

North Fork Trailhead was in a remote area of the Rocky Mountains, seven miles from Lost Falls, where Doug's parents did their research. They camped so far into backcountry that Doug and Gordon usually went the whole three weeks without seeing another human being.

Once they were settled in, it wasn't so bad, but Doug disliked the long routine of getting ready—the stop at Park Headquarters to pick up the research permit, the drive up Devil's Gulch Road to the unpaved road, to the trailhead, and then backpacking their supplies in on foot. There were two tents, a smaller pup tent, sleeping bags, pots and pans, the food, the Coleman stove, their clothes, the scientific equipment, and the empty plastic water jugs attached to each pack that thunked together with every step a person took.

They started out on the trail, but later veered off to reach a point above Lost Falls within a day's hike of the lakes, rivers, and streams of that area. In this isolated wilderness, the landmarks for five miles in any direction had names such as Mummy Mountain, Stormy Peaks, Icefield Pass, and Lost Lake Trail. Because the Grillos kept in shape, they usually made the hike in four hours.

The first few days were always the hardest—getting used to digging "cat-holes" again, for their toilets; washing with as little soap as possible; carrying and boiling water; counterbalancing their food from a tree limb; doing the same with their trash.

Because Mr. and Mrs. Grillo had a research grant from the Park Service, they did not have to move their tents to a new spot every few days as other hikers in backcountry had to do. Instead, they made camp at a place chosen by the area ranger, far off the trail, and usually on rock, so as to disturb the undergrowth as little as possible in any one place. Leave no trace of your visit to the wilderness, not even footprints, Dad always told them. The rules were time-consuming, even tedious. But then, when the three weeks were over, Doug was always sorry to go.

Glad and sorry, at the same time. Last summer, all Gordon did was bug him about going up there—to the place Doug wouldn't talk about. Gordon tried every which way to make him admit he was scared. The trick, Doug had decided this year, was to stay busy. Always busy. To be doing something every minute of the day, so that Gordon couldn't catch him off guard and ask, "Okay, Doug, why not now?"

It was close to dark when the tents were up at last, and the family celebrated with ham sandwiches on French bread, cheese and olives, and cookies and grapes from the supermarket. It would be three weeks, Doug knew, before he tasted food this good again.

"Well, what do you guys have planned this year?" Mother asked, hugging her knees. In her book, time had to be planned. That was okay with Doug.

"Merit badges," he said.

Both Doug and Gordon were Scouts, though now that Gordon was entering high school, he divided his time between camp-outs and track. The real motivation was a promise from Dad that when and if each of his sons reached the rank of Eagle Scout, the two of them—he and Dad—would go on a trip of Doug or Gordon's choosing: scuba diving off the Florida coast, perhaps. Spelunking in Pennsylvania. White-water rafting in Colorado. A whole week of fun. To earn the rank of Eagle meant a whole mess of merit badges, showing leadership ability, directing a service project—a lot of hard work. Dad wanted his sons strong. More than that, he wanted leaders.

"It's a tough world out there," he said, not once but often.

Gordon had made it to Star, two ranks below Eagle, while Doug was a rank below Star. Still, Doug was gaining. Wouldn't it be a blast if he beat Gordie to it, he fantasied, and imagined him and Dad leaving together on a scuba-diving vacation.

Now, in answer to his mom's question, Doug added, "I'm working on a badge in mammals."

Gordon snorted derisively, but Dad said, "That should be easy to do up here."

"I'll be working on one in orienteering," Gordon said. "Go get myself lost and see if I can find my way back by compass."

"That's a requirement?" asked Mother.

Gordon grinned. "No, but I'd like to try it."

"Be careful," Mother said.

Doug's friends were always amazed at the casual way she said that. Both his parents, as long as he could remember, let them do more than most kids could. He remembered once in particular when he and Gordon and some of the guys hitchhiked home from a basketball game, and his friends got grounded for a week.

"You want to be careful about hitchhiking," was all Mom had said when they'd told her.

And all Dad said now to Gordon was, "Let us know when you decide to try that."

Cuba. That was the way Doug explained his dad. When you lose some of your relatives trying to get out of a country—almost not making it yourself, when your family has to start all over again with nothing at all, and you have to work your way through college, a little hitchhiking didn't seem like much. Dad had worked on about every kind of job there was—bricklaying, ranching, construction, oil rigging—some of it dangerous. After all that, he pretty much figured his sons could take care of themselves, Doug decided.

As for Mom, he thought he could explain her, too. It probably had something to do with her being a daughter and not being allowed to do all the things her brothers did, especially Lloyd. She always talked about that, anyway. Both she and Dad were geologists, and she'd met him at MIT while doing research on earthquakes. Hitchhiking couldn't compete with earthquakes on the worry scale, that was Doug's guess.

For the last six months, however, Mom had been worrying about something else. Uncle Lloyd, the uncle Doug rarely saw, was dying of melanoma in Massachusetts. He could live for another month, the doctors said, or he could live for another year. It was hard to say. So the Grillos had decided to go to Colorado as planned.

"If it happens when we're in the Rockies," Mom had said back in May, when they'd discussed Uncle Lloyd's dying, "Tony and I are going to drive to Denver and catch a plane to Boston for the funeral. I don't know what to say about you two. You could come along if you like, but since plane fare is astronomical—especially on short notice—and you scarcely knew your uncle, I don't see the point."

"I'd probably stay," Gordon had told her.

"Me too," Doug had said.

Mother had sighed. "Well, we'll see when the time comes. Lloyd may live another six months, who knows? But if he dies, Tony and I *have* to go, guys. The family would never forgive me if we didn't."

That was all she said.

Mom was never very close to her brothers, that much Doug knew. He also remembered the day Uncle Lloyd got his fourth stripe and flew an airliner—Mother's ambition when she was young—she had simply pressed her lips together and said to Doug, "I will never, ever, tell you there is anything you can't do. I'll never do that to my children, Doug."

And she never did.

Right now, Mom was thinking of Uncle Lloyd herself. She was eating a handful of grapes and looking thoughtful. "Wonder how Lloyd's doing," she said to no one in particular.

"How are we going to know?" Doug asked. "If he dies, I mean."

"I talked to the park superintendent about it," Dad said. "If a call comes for us at Park Headquarters, he said he'd see if he couldn't send someone out on horseback, considering the circumstances."

Mother began cleaning up the food scraps and wrappers. "Well, I'm going to stay optimistic and assume the best. 'Don't borrow trouble,' my mother always said. Now, who's going to eat that last sandwich?"

Both Doug and Gordon reached for it at once.

It was amazing how quickly the four of them fell into the rhythm of the mountains. The first day or two, even Doug and Gordon were friends, searching out their favorite places: the fallen tree ladder across a creek, its stubby branches making great hand- and footholds; the high meadow where they sometimes saw deer in the early evening; the beaver lodge; the water hole; the shallow caves at the base of a cliff. . . .

And then Gordon ruined it all. "You going up on the ridge with me this year, or you chicken?" he asked.

"Why are you always bugging me about it?" Doug glared.

"Do it, and I won't."

"What's it to you?"

"I just want to see if you can."

"Why should I?"

"Just do it."

"When I'm ready," Doug said, and when Gordon veered left in the underbrush, Doug turned right and circled back to camp.

He had only been up on the ridge one heart-stopping, terrifying time, and that was enough. It was two years ago that Gordon had found the spot. He'd gone hiking early that morning, and come back in late afternoon with tales of a wonderful place where you could see for miles around. A waterfall, everything! They had to come!

Dad had got out a backcountry trail map and helped Gordon pinpoint the location the best he could.

"If you were up there northeast of Stormy Peaks, Gordon, you were in the Comanche Peak Wilderness area. That's national forest—out of the park. Pretty wild territory."

"You've got to see it!" Gordon said again.

The next morning they'd packed some food, some trail mix, filled their canteens, and set out. It was a three-hour hike to the rock face, and a two-hour climb after that. To look back meant to see nothing but sky behind you, and down by your feet, the ground was peeling away at a rapid clip. But it was not until the trees on the left disappeared, then the shrubs, that the sweat broke out on Doug's forehead. He'd found himself on a narrow ledge six hundred feet high, and the earth did not just peel away, it dropped. One slip of the foot and you did not roll, to be stopped eventually by trees or rocks. You fell to the canyon below.

With Gordon in the lead, his mother next, then Doug, then Dad, Doug had kept his eyes on his mother's hiking boots just ahead. Her feet seemed to find the way along the ledge like a deer. He stepped where she stepped, he clutched whatever her hand had held—roots or rocks or anything else that protruded from the cliff wall. Knowing that his father was just behind him, Doug had moved numbly, never once, after that first glance downward, allowing his eyes to stray off the edge of the path, measuring the width carefully with his eyes as it narrowed to three feet, then two and a half, and finally—in the narrowest place of all—only two feet wide.

Doug had wanted to call out, cry out, but his tongue wouldn't move. And finally, they were past the place, and as they took off their backpacks and exclaimed over the view, Doug realized that his shirt was soaked, his heart pounding so fiercely it was painful.

"Pretty narrow back there," Dad had said, taking a long drink of water from his canteen. "You sure this is the only route up here, Gordon?"

"I tried another way, but it was blocked," Gordon had said.

"Well, you've got some loose rocks to look out for. Have to be careful of those. When you come again, Gordon, watch it."

He had not said "if" but "when."

"What you've got to do," Mother added, "is look for hand-holds. Be sure you know where your feet are going and what you'll be holding on to before you take your next step."

They had found the place Gordon told them about—a triangular spot set back from the ridge, where you could see not only straight up the rock face—past the waterfall and the spindly trees that seemed to grow out of the rock—to the summit, but land for miles around. Dad even pointed out a long stretch of the North Fork of the Big Thompson River. But as they ate their lunch by the waterfall, Doug had felt nothing, tasted nothing, the terror of what was ahead all too vivid in his mind.

On the return trip, he had found himself second in line. This time Dad went first, then Doug, then Gordon and Mom. And this time his chest froze up. Needles seemed to penetrate the palms of his hands, the soles of his feet. His butt tightened, his breath came short.

"Go *on*," he had heard Gordon saying behind him, and only then realized he had stopped. One more step, his hand grasping a root that grew a foot or two out of the rocks, and suddenly he flattened himself against the rock face.

"What's the matter?" Gordon had asked.

"I—c-can't," was all Doug could say.

"You've got to," Gordon told him. "It's the only way back. I've checked."

"Can't." It had taken all his strength to say even that word.

"Listen, Doug! You've got ten inches between you and the edge. Go *on*!"

No. Couldn't move. Couldn't breathe.

"Boys?" Mom's voice came from around the bend behind them. Dad's whistle up ahead.

"Doug's freaked out!" Gordon had yelled. "He won't move."

"C'mon, Doug. One foot at a time," his dad called.

Doug had closed his eyes. Dizzy. Too dizzy to walk. He could see his foot going over the edge. Almost feel it slipping. Knew that if he tried to walk, some unseen force would propel him over.

Then the sound of Dad's slow footsteps coming back, around the curve of the wall, the wide short-fingered hand, reaching out, grabbing his sleeve, Doug's hand grappling for Dad's, seizing it, and then slowly, sidestepping their way along the ledge, Doug's breath coming in loud nervous gasps, they reached the place where the path widened, and Doug threw up.

Gordon's eyes were laughing, but Mom and Dad wanted to talk about it.

"The best thing to do when something like this happens, Doug, is go back and do it again," Dad had said. "Show yourself who's boss. Don't let fear get a grip on you."

Doug had rinsed his mouth with water and spit it out, saying nothing.

"You want to go back and try that ledge again, just the two of us? I'll be right behind you."

"No!" Doug almost shouted the word.

They had sat there quietly for a moment or two, and then Mom said, "I was afraid of water once. Deep water. Somebody pushed me into a pool and I went under. It was almost a year before I was able to try the deep end of a swimming pool again. I wish someone had made me go back in the water right then."

In answer, Doug stood up, slipped on his shoulder pack once more, and started back down the mountain.

"Feeling better?" Mom had asked, catching up to him, as though it had not been a matter of courage at all, but a minor stomach upset.

Doug had nodded because he knew the worst was over, not only for now but forever. He would never go up there again. Of that he'd been certain.

CHAPTER 4

HE ASKED A QUESTION THAT EVENING HE HAD NOT ASKED BEFORE. Gordon and Dad had gone to refill the water jugs, and Doug was helping Mom clean up.

"Why didn't we ever visit Uncle Lloyd? We only saw him a couple times at reunions and stuff."

It was the first time Doug felt he had caught her off guard. "He never invited us," she said, finally.

Doug went on picking up scraps, dropping them in a plastic garbage bag, but then he had another question. "Was it that he didn't like you or you didn't like him?"

"I'm not sure it was a question of liking. . . ." Mother's hand moved jerkily as she wiped off the portable stove. She was wearing shorts and one of Dad's old shirts, knotted at the waist. "Our scruffy look," she always said of the way they dressed on camping trips.

"*What*, then?" Doug waited.

Mrs. Grillo spoke slowly, thinking over each word, it seemed. "He was the oldest, I was next in line. He was also very smart . . . and knew it. I don't think he once missed being on the honor roll—a track star, basketball player. Everything Dad wanted him to be, he was."

She stopped, as though that's all there was to the story.

"So?" Doug asked, urging her on.

"I never . . . he never allowed me my moment of glory. Do you know what I mean, Doug? No matter what I tried or accomplished, Lloyd would turn right around and do it better. And Dad praised him to the skies."

"Then what?"

"I don't know what. It just seemed as though one thing piled on top of another, until there were layers of . . . of grudges, I guess. So many layers we never did get to the bottom of it. Maybe it was Dad's fault for favoring the boys. For pitting us against each other. Perhaps that's who I'm really angry with. Who knows?"

"Then why take it out on Lloyd?"

"Who said I took it out on him?" There was an edge to her voice now.

"You never called him."

"I'm not the only one capable of picking up the phone."

"Did we ever invite him to see us?"

"No."

Doug fell silent. He hoisted the garbage bag high in the air again, where it dangled over the limb of a cottonwood. "Don't you want to see him before he dies?" he asked, finally.

"I did see him. I was in Boston last month, remember?"

"I thought you were visiting your sister."

"Well, I was. But I saw Lloyd briefly. We said our good-byes. We just weren't *close*, Doug. You can't *make* yourself like someone."

"Sort of like Gordie and me," Doug said.

Mother turned around. "No, *not* like Gordon and you!" She studied him intently. "Whatever made you say that?"

Doug shrugged. "I don't know. After we're grown up, I can't see me going to visit him much, either."

"Doug, what an awful thing to say!" Mother put down her sponge and her face was earnest. "I want you guys to be close. We've always taken you on vacations together, you both belong to Scouts, you . . ."

"We're different, Mom."

"Not *that* different. Listen, Doug, after Dad and I are gone, there's only going to be one other person who remembers the things you do now, who shared so much of your life when you were young, and that's Gordon. Don't forget it."

Doug didn't answer. How different did you have to be to be enemies? he wondered. How much alike to be friends?

The conversation at mealtime was mostly about the Grillos' work. For the past four summers, Doug's parents had been monitoring the water and soil in the rugged northeast corner of Rocky Mountain National Park to see what effect acid rain might be having on the lakes and streams, rock and soil. The Park Service was reintroducing the greenback trout to the area, and it was important the water stay pollution-free. Water samples had to be taken every mile or half mile, beginning at the source, if possible. Getting their containers into the area was no problem, but once they were full, the Grillos would need a horse to carry them back out again. The ranger would see to that.

Sometimes Doug or Gordon went with their parents on their field expeditions to Lost Lake or Lake Husted, but usually the brothers preferred staying behind and exploring, each on his own.

Now they had been there four days when Dad called to them one evening: "Come here! Want to show you something."

Doug and Gordon went with him down the slope toward the stream, walking beside, rather than behind, him, the way Dad had taught them, so as not to trample the undergrowth into any sort of path. But Dad didn't stop at the stream bank. He followed it on past the beaver lodge, to the low area they called the watering hole. There, in the thin layer of mud, were tracks. Not hoof tracks—not deer or elk—but not bear prints either. Doug knew bear tracks.

"Yeah?" said Gordon. "What do you think they are?"

"I don't know. Seem pretty big for a bobcat," Dad told him, bending over to take a close look.

"Mountain lion?" asked Gordon.

Dad shook his head. "Could be, but I don't think there are many in the park."

"There was something about them on the bulletin board in Park Headquarters," Gordon said.

"There are warnings in Park Headquarters about a lot of things you'll never see. Cougars keep to themselves," Dad told him.

"Well, it's got to be one or the other," said Doug. "That's a cat's print."

"A *grand*daddy of a bobcat, that's my guess," his father said. "Keep an eye out, maybe you'll see it."

Doug lagged behind to study the print. He guessed a cougar. Boy, wouldn't he love to get a photo.

He spent the next three days spying on the water hole. If he woke up early, he'd go down before breakfast. He'd go at dusk. And always he walked so quietly he hardly moved a twig—made a practice of it: Indian walking, he called it. Not a sound. Glide over the ground as though it were water. He saw a few deer, a moose and a moose calf, possums. But the cougar was never there.

"If it was a cougar, it was probably passing through," his father told him when Doug brought it up again. "Idaho. Now that's where you'll find the cougars."

Doug gave up then, and worked on trying to get a picture of a deer.

"Take good pictures of two kinds of mammals in the wild," the requirements in his Scout manual read. "Record light conditions, film used, exposure, and other factors, including notes on the activities of the pictured animals."

Also: "Spend three hours of each of five days on at least a twenty-five acre area. List the mammal species you identified by sight or sound."

This would take some doing. He'd love to get a photo of a beaver, but they came out at night, and he wasn't sure he'd brought the right film.

"You still working on the wimp badge?" Gordon asked him one evening as he lay on his sleeping bag, listening to his Walkman.

"You're such a wonder, how come you did Leatherwork?" Doug retorted. Why did he fall into these traps? But he kept on.

"How come you did Insect Study?" He let his voice rise delicately on the words, *Insect Study*.

"You have a problem with that?"

That's the way it always went. Gordon would start something and when Doug gave back as good as he got, Gordon would say, "You have a problem with that?" or "Think you're smart?" and before you knew it, there would be a fight. Why didn't *Doug* ever remember to say, "You have a problem with that?"

"Yeah, I have a problem with that," Doug said, barreling on. "The guy who's always talking big is going to stand up in front of the troop and get his 'buggie badge.' Gordie's gonna get a badge with a big bad cricket on it."

"You're gonna get a little squirrel on yours, so why are you spouting off?"

Doug couldn't hold back. He had a trump card he'd been saving, and decided to play it now. "You know those envelopes you mailed out for Mom? About the Court of Honor? You know those stamps you promised to put on?"

Gordon glanced over quickly.

"You know how you were complaining they were all stuck together? Well, that's because I sprinkled pee on them and let them dry."

He made for an opening in the tent, but Gordon tackled him and the fight was on. And all the while Doug was yelling he was laughing, too. He didn't even mind the punches. Got some in himself. Just the thought of Gordon licking those peed-on stamps was worth it.

Usually their parents let them fight things out. Gordon's punches were quicker, but Doug hit harder. In any case, they always stopped short of homicide. This time, however, Mother's voice came shouting over the scuffle: "Damn it, I want this stopped!"

It was not the way she usually talked. Not the way at all.

Doug pulled his leg off Gordon. His elbow was bleeding.

"Like *animals*!" Mother was standing at the door of the tent now. Her voice seemed to fill up all the space in the clearing. "We come out here to give you boys an experience that most kids would give anything to have, and you spend it fighting with each other. I'm *sick* of the quarreling. Sick to death of this ridiculous, idiotic, insane bickering over the slightest little thing!"

"Doug just told me . . . ," Gordon began.

"I don't want to *hear* what Doug told you. I want peace. I have enough on my mind without this. Do you understand?" Her voice was shrill.

"Yes," Doug answered.

Gordon nodded.

She stalked off toward the woods then, and Doug noticed that her chin trembled. Were they really that bad? It had to be more than just the fight. They'd fought dozens of times before, a lot worse than this, too. Her worry over Uncle Lloyd, no doubt. The outburst probably didn't have much to do with them at all.

Gordon, however, still furious, took Doug's backpack and overturned it onto the ground. Underpants, T-shirts, half-worn socks rolled up in balls, sweat shirts . . .

Doug didn't try to stop him, didn't even go over and empty out his. Just waited until Gordon had stomped outside, then tore a page out of his notebook and in big letters, wrote GORDIE LICKS PEE, and laid it on Gordon's sleeping bag.

CHAPTER 5

GORDON WENT UP INTO THE NATIONAL FOREST THE NEXT DAY.

Doug watched him go. He knew that his brother liked to sleep outside at night—alone, if he had to—but Scout camp-outs were his favorite. To Gordie, it was fun lying in an open pup tent while a dozen mosquitoes tried to find his face. Fun to cram his bedroll in beside a bunch of other guys, all trying to see who could fart loudest and smell up the place. To Doug, camp-outs were okay, but he liked working on merit badges. Liked having something to show for his work.

"So," Dad used to say, "there's something for each of you."

If he had known, as a boy back in Cuba, the things Doug and

Gordon had learned so far, Dad told them, he would have known that it didn't have to be terribly cold for a man to die of hypothermia—that any combination of cool weather, damp clothes, wind, exhaustion, and hunger could do it. Who would have thought that on the warm coastal waters off Cuba, one of his uncles would die in their desperate attempt to reach the Florida coast?

"Learn to depend on yourself," he told the boys.

Make do. Mom's favorite line.

So Gordon went up past the Fear Place once or twice each summer by himself and stayed overnight. To tell the truth, Doug liked it better when he was gone. There was no "ridiculous, idiotic, insane bickering," for one thing.

The task Doug had given himself for this particular day was to find a hiding place in the high meadow that he could use as a blind, so he could watch animals undetected. Maybe get some photos. He searched until he found a spot just at the edge of the meadow, with a large rock he could sit on, hidden completely from view by foliage.

He'd brought some crackers and a packet of juice, and he waited, but mostly what he saw were birds. Heck, those he could have seen if he'd just stretched out on his back in the grass! But then he saw an eagle—saw it soaring, saw it swoop, heard the terrified cry of a jackrabbit as the talons gouged, then saw the eagle fly up toward the mountain with the rabbit, limp and bloody, beneath.

Doug wondered if the eagle's nest was somewhere up near Gordie—if Gordie was watching the eagle, too.

He was trying not to think about what it would be like to be up in that camping spot with Gordon. Maybe not with Gordon exactly, but high enough that he could see a whole lot more than he could here.

He remembered climbing with his father once in the desert— over wider trails he could manage—and looking down on the ground below to see wind spouts, which seemed to hover for a while over a spot here and there, sending up dust in a little swirl, like smoke from a campfire, then moving on.

And now, remembering the waterfall in the place where Gordon was, the way it tumbled into a shallow, rocky pool, he thought, too, of how he and Gordon could have horsed around in the water. Wondered if Gordon was up there having fun all by himself—whether he felt the same.

When Gordon came back the next day, he came with stories of having scaled an even higher ridge than the one he had scaled before. He'd come upon an eagle's nest, and had been able to look over once and see the young. "I saw the mother bring a rabbit," Gordon said.

"Yeah, well you should have been down where I was," Doug said excitedly. "I saw her swoop and catch it."

"No, you should have been up at the top. Man, you can see out over the whole country, practically. You should come, Doug."

"I will when I'm good and ready," Doug replied.

"Which is never, right?"

Doug saw Mother looking at them, her eyebrows inching closer to each other, and made no reply.

It was late afternoon when they heard the hoofbeats, the snort of a horse, and then a big brown animal trotted into the clearing, turning its head to one side as the ranger brought it to a stop.

Dad went over and took a note from the man, passing it on to Mother. No one said anything as she carried it into her tent, but then the ranger lifted a large brown grocery sack from his saddlebag, handing it to Gordon.

"Thought I'd bring a little cheer along with the bad news," he said. "Met some campers back at the trailhead who wanted to unload some groceries, so I figured I'd give them to you. Make a nice breakfast tomorrow, maybe."

Doug went over and peeked in the sack. A carton of eggs, half a package of bacon, orange juice, pancake mix, syrup, grapefruit, bananas, coffee . . .

"Somebody was carrying this stuff in a backpack?" Doug asked incredulously.

The ranger smiled. "Takes all kinds . . . ," he said.

"Stay and have dinner with us?" Father invited.

"I'd like to, but I've got things I have to tend to before dark." The ranger looked toward Mother's tent. "I'm sorry about her brother. Headquarters called me at the patrol cabin this afternoon with the news. Anything else I can do?"

Dad shook his head. "No. We've got some decisions to make, that's all."

The ranger nodded and turned his horse around.

CHAPTER 6

EARLY THE NEXT MORNING, FROM THE BASE OF AN ASPEN, DOUG watched his parents pack for the trip to Boston. It wasn't until he heard his mother mention "my blue dress back in the car" that he realized his parents had come here prepared for Uncle Lloyd's death, and had left their good clothes at the trailhead, in case.

The evening before, after the news had come, Doug had happened upon his mother unexpectedly. Not realizing that she had gone to the stream, Doug had taken two of the jugs himself and set off down the slope. He had almost stepped out of the trees when he heard her sobbing, and stood unmoving where he was.

He had rarely seen his mother cry except for last summer

when she'd hurt her back, and once when all of them had not only forgotten Mother's Day, but had made a mess of the kitchen as well. But yesterday, standing in the trees with the water jugs and seeing his mother crouched there by the stream, hands over her face, shoulders shaking, Doug had felt he was invading her privacy, barging in on feelings she hadn't wanted to share. He'd gone back to camp again as quietly as he'd come. And when she returned with the water, her face composed, only a telltale wetness of her eyelashes, she had said nothing, shared nothing, given no clue as to what she'd been feeling down by the water. Would it be so awful, Doug had wondered, to just let go and grieve for Lloyd?

Now Doug waited for them to leave, hating that awkward moment when they'd say good-bye. They had the long hike back to the trailhead before them, a trip to the public showers to clean up, then the drive to Denver, and finally the flight to Boston.

"Tony, do you think we're wise to leave the boys by themselves?" Doug heard his mother say to Dad from inside their tent.

"We've left them overnight before when we were out in the field," Dad replied. "They did fine. Better campers in some ways than we are."

"I'd feel better if someone knew they were here alone, though."

"Then we'll find a ranger on our way out and tell him."

Now they were getting a later start than they'd hoped, and Doug wished they'd just go. They couldn't even be sure till they got to town and called Denver whether they could get seats on a flight tonight or not.

When his parents came out of the tent, Mother hastily slipped on her backpack. Doug knew he should say something to her, but wasn't sure what. That it was good Uncle Lloyd had not suffered too long? He didn't know that. That at least he'd had a good life? That he knew Mom would miss him? He wasn't sure of anything.

Finally he just said, "I'm sorry about Uncle Lloyd, Mom," and she gave him a big hug.

"So am I," she said. "I can't say I'm looking forward to this. . . . What I dread the most, strangely, is what to say to my father." She sighed. And then, to both of them, "You guys stick together now. There's not a whole lot of food, but certainly enough to last till we come back, and we'll bring a load of groceries with us. Tony was planning to go to Park Headquarters even if this hadn't happened and tell them we'll be here for another week or so anyway."

"You know the rules," Dad said. "We'll tell the ranger you're here by yourselves, so don't be surprised if he looks in on you. And you'll need to boil more water. We're low."

"We'll take care of everything," said Gordon. "How long will you be gone?"

"Only two nights. Possibly three. We'll try to get a late flight out of Denver. If I can, I want to apply for a grant at the university while I'm in Boston. The funeral's tomorrow afternoon, and we'll catch an early flight back Thursday if we can. Be in camp before dark, if we're lucky. Don't worry, though, if we're not here before Friday, in case we have trouble booking seats."

Their feet made almost no sound as they started off. If Doug had closed his eyes, he wouldn't even have known they had gone. He watched the bobbing of their heads, and returned their wave just before they disappeared into the trees.

Gordon sat down on a log outside their tent and whacked idly at it with a long stick. *Whack, whack, whack.* Small pieces of bark flew in every direction, the stick growing shorter and shorter. The bony knobs of Gordon's shoulder bones moved back and forth beneath his T-shirt. Just like Mom, he didn't seem to put on weight no matter what he ate.

"So what do you want to do?" he asked finally.

Doug shrugged. "I don't know." He was quiet a moment. "Mom was really upset," he added. He wasn't sure he wanted to tell Gordie about her crying, though.

Gordon glanced over at him. "She hardly ever saw Uncle Lloyd."

"You still care when somebody dies, though."

"Yeah, I guess so."

They both hung around camp that morning. The air was warmer than it usually got this high up in the Rockies. The boys sprawled on the ground, their backs against the log, trading comic books and watching for the marmot that lived in the rocks.

About one-thirty they scrounged around for something to eat. Mother had made a gourmet breakfast that morning from the food the ranger had given them—all the luxuries they'd been doing without. They'd eaten till they were stuffed. But now the meal was wearing off, or perhaps it was only boredom setting in, but Doug and Gordon were hungry again.

Lunch, however, was a real disappointment. There was enough food to last until Mom and Dad came back, all right, but not the boys' favorites, and most of what was left had to be cooked.

They haggled over the remaining treats. Doug took the sardines, so Gordon took the graham crackers and peanut butter.

"Gordon!" Doug said. "You can't have them both."

"You got the sardines."

"Fifty-fifty," said Doug, so they opened the tin, counted them out, and divided the one extra.

Nothing they ate seemed to satisfy them, however. At two o'clock, Doug found Gordon eating the cheese, just wolfing it down.

"You'd better stop it, Gordon!" he yelled. "You're eating everything up, and this has to last through Thursday."

"So I'm eating my share now," Gordon told him. "What do you care?"

They finally cooked up the last packet of chili Mexicana.

What was unsettling to Doug was that they were both hungry again at three, as though nothing at all would fill them up. They lowered the food bag once again and ate crackers and jelly.

The sack the grand breakfast had come in stood propped against one of the tents, filled to overflowing with the bacon wrapping, an orange juice container, grapefruit rinds, a pancake box, banana peels. . . .

"You'd better take care of the garbage, Gordon," Doug told him. "It's beginning to stink."

"It's not my turn; I did it yesterday."

"That's a lie, Gordon! *I* did!"

"Don't be stupid, Doug. It's your turn, and I'm not going to do it."

Doug stood in the middle of the clearing, his temperature rising, fists clenched, as Gordon sprawled on the grass again with a crossword puzzle, his head against the log. It was understood that he and Gordon were to take turns at kitchen duty—scraping off plates, rinsing everything in hot water, flattening the cans, lowering the refuse bag from the tree to dump the stuff in. It would be taken into town, at last, when they left. Other jobs could slide by for a day or two, but no one dared leave garbage around.

Doug felt his jaws tense. "You stink-head! You'd better!"

"Well, I won't! It's not my turn!"

Doug kicked at the log, making Gordon's head jerk, then kicked it again as hard as he could.

"Cut it out, Doug."

He had known it was going to be this way after the folks left. Gordon would get out of doing everything. Doug didn't know if his stomach hurt because he was hungry or because he was angry. White-hot fire stabbed at his temples. His jaw felt like a nutcracker. Tying up garbage was the worst job of all. Every time you opened the bag to add more, you got a face full of stink. It was *Gordon's turn*! He *wouldn't* do it! Still, it had to be done.

He clomped over to his parents' tent, grabbed the paper sack, and headed toward the trees. The sack was damp and smelly, and one corner was already wearing through.

Anger was a ball of heat in his throat. As he passed Gordon on the ground, he swung the bag sideways, just to bump him a bit. The banana peels, bacon wrapping, and grapefruit rinds rained down on Gordon's chest, dropping in smelly clumps onto his lap.

Gordon stared, aghast—arms held out away from him. "Doug, you scumbag!" Instantly he was on his feet.

Dazed at first by the breakage of the sack, Doug's jaw dropped, but just as suddenly, adrenaline poured through his body and he was fighting off the fury of his brother.

A tangle of arms and legs, a blur of bodies on the ground. Fists pummeling, knees poking, feet kicking . . . Doug felt his lip split open, a stabbing pain in his side, a kick on his shin, and then suddenly Gordon rolled off and sat breathing heavily some distance away, eyes wild and angry, scrapes and bruises on his hands and face. Doug, too, sat panting, glaring, getting his breath back, ready to take another tumble, but then Gordon stood up. Without a word, he went inside their tent.

Doug went over to the cottonwood and sat down, rubbing a scratch on his arm. His tongue felt thick and swollen, and there was a cut on his knee.

He *was* glad the garbage bag had broken. It would be a mess to clean up, of course, but it was worth it to see the look on Gordie's face when all that slop fell in his lap. He put one hand to his lip. It was bleeding.

Already he felt they had let their parents down. Dad and Mom hadn't even been gone a day and already he and Gordon had had a fight. That had *never* happened before.

He could hear movement inside the tent. An occasional thump or thud. Gordon would try to get even, that's for sure. He was probably going to take all Doug's clothes down to the stream and throw them in.

Should he go in the tent and stop him? Doug knew that's what Gordon wanted. No, he wouldn't say anything. *Let* him put all his clothes in the stream. They'd still be there when Mom came back. Doug could go a week in the clothes he was wearing if he had to.

Ten minutes later Gordon came out with his pack and sleeping bag. He didn't even look at Doug—just hauled down the line holding the food.

Doug watched silently, heart thumping. He hadn't expected this. Gordon wasn't supposed to leave. It was understood. Always understood that if it was just the two of them, Gordon was in charge. You guys stick together, Mom had said. He was just doing this to spite him, Doug knew. Just doing it to get even.

Gordon was spreading all the food packets out on the ground. Doug started to get up, to make sure he didn't take more than his share, then stopped. From where he sat, it looked as though Gordon were dividing everything fifty-fifty. He had to admit he was surprised.

He said nothing at all as Gordon stuffed his share into a canvas bag, nothing at all as Gordon added a half-gallon jug of water, and neither said a word as Gordon slipped on his backpack and started out in the direction of Comanche Peak Wilderness.

Suddenly, however, Doug leaped to his feet and hauled down the food again. Quickly he rummaged through the packets. *All* the trail mix was gone. All the applesauce, the graham crackers, the peanut butter. The coconut macaroon mix had disappeared. Also the cereal. There was scarcely anything left that didn't have to be cooked.

"Gordon, you bring that stuff back!" he bellowed.

The figure kept on going, getting smaller and smaller in the distance.

IT DIDN'T MATTER MUCH. DOUG COULD GET BY WITH THE DEHYDRATED stuff. He figured the reason Gordon hadn't taken *all* the food was that he couldn't carry it. No, maybe that was wrong. Gordon hadn't even taken the best of everything, only the things he could fix without a stove.

Well, great! Doug would have a day and night to himself, then. He'd like that just fine.

As he cleaned up the mess on the ground, he thought again of the fight. He may have a split lip, but at least he got in some good punches of his own. Gordon deserved everything he got. Just because the folks were gone, he thought he could get away with anything. How could he sit right there and say it wasn't his turn to tie up the garbage? He'd look right at you and lie to your face!

Doug had tied up the garbage on Monday, Wednesday, Friday, and Sunday. . . . Wednesday, Friday, Sunday, and . . . . This was Tuesday. Doug swallowed. Wednesday, Friday, Sunday, Tuesday. . . . For crying out loud, it *was* his turn! He let out his breath and stared out across the field where Gordon had disappeared.

Well, heck, so he was wrong. Why didn't Gordon tell him? Why did he just keep repeating that he'd tied up the garbage the day before? Why didn't he name the days it was Doug's turn, and then Doug would have realized he'd made a mistake. Anyone could make a mistake. Gordie must have been looking for a fight, that's all. They could have settled it peacefully if Gordie had tried halfway. But that's how Gordon was.

It was the first time Doug had ever had the camp all to himself. What he noticed most was the quiet—so heavy he could almost touch it. Maybe an insect noise now and then, or the sound of the wind in the trees—a long crescendo of *shhhhh*, sometimes stopping abruptly, other times dying out into nothingness.

He decided to go to the high meadow and see if he could get more photos. It was late afternoon, and he might just stay until dusk, see if any deer showed up.

Taking his notebook and camera, he set out up the rocky hill, with switchbacks that took him around a bend and then onto higher ground.

A climb like this, Doug could manage, even though it was strenuous as he made his way over the boulders. Here, a slip of the foot or a fall might mean a good long roll over the rocks; it might mean a broken arm or leg, a cracked collarbone, cuts and bruises, but it did not mean that, once over the edge, you were gone, your life a blip, snuffed out in a space of ten seconds.

Ahead of him, the far mountains rose in layers. Sometimes the closest ridge was in sunlight, the rest in shadow. But as the clouds shifted, the middle range came into focus. There were times Doug couldn't see any of them at all.

Just like the ocean, Mom said. Always changing.

To his left, bright orange lichen grew on the trunks of trees, and on the sides of some of the rocks. New trees claimed spaces among old ones. Dead trees stood almost limbless, their bark shiny and bare, silver-swirled.

He began the steeper part of the climb. There was no wind that he could detect, but he knew from which direction it came when it did, for the trees had only stubs of limbs on their exposed sides.

As he climbed, he passed a waterfall that served as a conduit for castaway trees. The path of the falls and the base itself was cluttered with the trunks of alders and aspens, bare of branches, and large moon-white limbs, piled in slapdash fashion, as though some giant hand had been playing pick-up sticks with them, holding them upright, then letting them fall where they would. Where the water foamed and splashed on the rocks, a water ouzel walked right under the spray, searching for insects.

Twenty minutes later, Doug came out upon the high meadow. He went immediately to the place he had chosen for his observatory, but though he sat quietly for an hour, he saw only a chipmunk. In past summers he'd seen plenty of deer, a moose or two, lots of smaller animals.

He thought again of Gordon up on the rock face, up near the

eagle's nest. Wondered if he had taken a camera with him. Darn Gordie, anyway. He *had* wanted a fight. Doug mulled it over again and again. He *could* have explained it to Doug, but he just kept saying "I did it yesterday!" like a stupid parrot or something.

In disgust, Doug finally got up off the rock, gathered his things together, and left. He could have gotten more pictures at home than he was getting here.

He set off down the hill. Going back down a steep grade was always harder for him than climbing up. He had good muscles in his thighs. It was his knees and shins that took the punishment when he went down a climb, his toes pressing against the ends of his sneakers. The sun was lower now. He looked at his watch. 6:30.

Something, Doug did not know what, made him feel uneasy. Worry about Gordon? That didn't seem to be it. The air was still of all birdcalls, all insect noises—a dead kind of silence. Without knowing how he knew, Doug had the troubled sense that he was being followed.

He stopped and looked around. His eye surveyed every tree, every bush—slowly scanning, like a camera. Nothing. He moved forward again, passing the waterfall, stepping over the rocks that jutted up out of the path at odd angles.

The feeling didn't go away. There was the distinct feeling that he was not alone, and that from somewhere close by, he was being observed.

He had never felt threatened here before, and—except for the Fear Place—never thought that his life might be in danger. A trickle of sweat traced his spine, icy cold, and caught at last in the waistband of his shorts.

Doug had reached the woods now, and as he made his way

along the shadowed path, he suddenly heard a twig snap off to his left. Then silence. He stood stone still.

Gordie. He felt a sweep of relief. It was probably all a hoax, his pretending to go off for the night. Doug bet that as soon as Gordon was out of sight, he had backtracked around to camp just to see if he could scare the daylights out of Doug for a day or two. Howls in the night. A footprint here, a noise there. Just exactly the kind of thing Gordon would do.

He almost yelled, "Okay, Gordie, I know it's you." But he didn't. What stopped him?

Doug began walking again, half smiling to himself. This could be fun. All the while Gordie was spying on him, he'd be spying on Gordie. Wouldn't it be a riot if some night he sneaked up on Gordie as he was stalking the tent and tackled him from behind? Heart-attack city!

Now, out of the corner of his eye, he saw a blur of movement off to his right, dodging from tree to tree, and jerked his head.

C'mon, Gordie, he thought. You can do better than that.

And then he saw it, the tawny flash of color, the quivering tail: *cougar.*

CHAPTER 8

I'M DEAD. IT WAS THE FIRST THOUGHT IN DOUG'S MIND. HE WAS HERE by himself, still a mile from camp, with absolutely nothing he could use to defend himself.

Play dead. His next thought. That was what he'd heard you do with a grizzly bear if you can't get away. Just as quickly as the idea came, however, Doug discarded it. Lie down now, and he'd be breakfast, lunch, and dinner for the big cat.

Out of the corner of his eye, he could see the small head, the long, sleek body, quivering tail. Any moment the animal would spring. Should he just go limp? Don't panic. Cats can detect panic.

Yet fear was filling his body like water seeping into his lungs. He could almost feel the place, the very spot in his chest or stomach, where it erupted, flowing through his veins and making his fingers ice cold.

Fear begat fear. One thought tumbled over another as he watched the cougar pause. He would be killed—his body mangled and mauled right here on the path. His face half eaten. Then Gordie would come back and the cougar would kill him, too. Mom and Dad would return to find both of their sons dead.

Well, don't just stand here. Still another thought, as though he were two selves now—one, the terrified kid who stood paralyzed on the path, the other his wiser self, taking over the controls, setting him on automatic.

He thought of what he had read about confronting a hostile dog. Avoid eye contact, he remembered that. Let the animal see your profile. Keep both hands in sight.

He did all three, shakily walking forward once again in as measured a pace as possible, belying the terror that tickled his throat, heart pounding against his rib cage. Whenever the animal moved ahead a few paces, Doug could see it without turning. Though not as huge as a jungle lion, it was big to Doug—five or six feet from its nose to the tip of its tail, he guessed. The jaws looked as strong as a steel-trap, and the paws seemed unusually large.

Doug felt an almost uncontrollable urge to pee but he didn't dare. Had to keep going. The pounding in his chest seemed unnatural. Was he having a heart attack? Maybe people didn't die of animal bites at all. Maybe they had heart attacks first, and then the big cats sprung. Fear upon fear upon fear. Go on, he told his feet.

Was the cougar trying to get ahead of him so it could turn around and meet him face-to-face on the trail? Was it going to maneuver itself closer so as to squeeze Doug against a rocky wall? When two or three minutes had passed, however, and the cougar had not attacked, Doug put his mind solely on reaching camp. He would have to make peace with a heartbeat that was out of control, but the main thing was to keep his feet moving. Keep the same pace. Don't let up.

Strangely, the cougar seemed not to be trying very hard to stay hidden. It certainly was not like the lions portrayed in *National Geographic* specials, their bellies almost touching the ground as they moved stealthily through the brush toward an unsuspecting flock of gazelles. The cougar was more like a dog bounding through the woods.

It was the clearing Doug dreaded now. The cougar might want to get him out in the open, away from trees where he'd try to hide. It was waiting for Doug to move out into open space, and then it would close in for the kill. Doug's body was drenched in sweat.

And yet, strangest of all, when Doug reached camp and took a tentative step out into the clearing, the cat went only a few feet into the fading sunshine, made a U-turn, and darted back into the trees, disappearing completely from view.

Doug did not stop, pause, or even look back. It was only when he was inside his tent that he dared turn around, his breathing coming in short, fractured little breaths.

The cougar was gone.

He let out an audible sigh and sank to the ground, his legs suddenly spaghetti beneath him. And then, when his breathing returned to normal, he crawled over and sat in the opening, trying to sort out what had happened.

It had been a cougar, all right—his feet about the size of the paw prints they had found at the water hole. Doug had a mental image of it making that U-turn, and the more he thought, the more it seemed to be frolicking. Or was Doug just trying to reassure himself?

He ventured out finally, far enough to pee, then sat on the log, looking all around him—right and left, turning every so often to check behind. He had read that sometimes cougar cubs, who have lost their mothers and are fed by humans for a while, may return to the family from time to time. Was it possible that someone in this area had taken care of a cub or cubs before leaving the park, and this is what kept the cougar here? That something had happened to its mother, and this cougar stayed behind?

The fear he had felt earlier turned to frank amazement that he was okay. But did he dare stray from camp tomorrow? That was the question.

It took him twenty minutes to make dinner that night. He'd looked everything over, and it was only beans and rice that appealed to him. If Mom were here, she would have added the green peas packet and probably made the raspberry cobbler, but Doug wasn't that ambitious, and didn't like raspberry.

He sat on the log a long time after dinner, watching the woods and the very spot in the clearing where the cougar had stepped so briefly out of the trees. He saw nothing more. After dark, he bathed—his armpits were beginning to smell—and realized there was only a half jug of water left that had been boiled. Thanks, Gordie.

He spent the evening boiling water. The Grillos used a simple system of collecting water from the stream in unmarked jugs, boiling it on the stove, then pouring it into plastic jugs marked with an X. Doug knew better than to drink from the unmarked jugs. Water from mountain streams was deceptively clear; cold, sparkling, and dangerous. It often carried a disease that caused intestinal cramps and vomiting, and no serious camper took chances unless it was an emergency. Sometimes, when they went hiking all day, the family took along a water filter instead of jugs. But boiling was best.

As Doug worked, he tried not to think of his stomach because he was hungry again. That was the best way to get by in the mountains; try not to think of food.

About one in the morning, Doug woke in a cold sweat. He lay with his eyes wide open, entirely motionless, heart thumping. Didn't even blink. He had thought he heard a noise, a growl, but the more he mulled it over, the more he was convinced he had dreamed it, because he had also seen eyes glistening in the dark, yet the tent flap was closed and zipped. That much he *had* dreamed.

He dreamed that a cougar was crouched at the foot of his sleeping bag in the attack position—tail quivering, haunches tense, eyes huge and yellow in the blackness. Doug lay quietly as his heartbeat returned to normal. He did not feel relaxed, however. Something else he'd read, perhaps?

Then he remembered—seemed to see a photo of a woman and a cougar in a magazine. A newspaper, maybe, at school. As he lay in the darkness, the story came slowly back to memory in pieces. It was a story about a woman who had gone out in her yard in Estes Park about midnight to hang up damp clothes, and a cougar had brushed against her legs. Yes, that was the story he was thinking of.

So what was scary about that? That should be even more reassuring.

He tried to let the story unfold, let the computer of his mind go on the search-and-find mode. Okay. She said she had stroked its throat. He remembered that, too. The cougar had rubbed against her legs, and she'd stroked its throat. Doug thought the story also might have said that the cougar purred. Or did he only imagine that?

There was more, but it was fuzzy. The woman had let the cougar into her house and fed it, but it never ventured beyond the kitchen. Doug remembered that, too.

"Stupid fool thing for her to do!" Dad had said when Doug read the article to him. "Wild animals are *not* pets, and people just can't get that into their heads. They think a young lion wants to romp with them, and the next thing you know they're mauled to death."

And then Doug remembered the line that had caused him to waken—had caused his heart to thunk and his palms to sweat: She had never turned her back on it, the woman had said in the story. I watch its eyes to tell if it's reverting to a wild state. Yes, that was it.

Well, never mind, because he was here in the tent and there wasn't any cougar to watch. And even when he wasn't inside, his manual on mammals said that cougars rarely attacked humans. Having pinned down the cause of his wariness, Doug slept, but only fitfully, and finally got up at five when the first pink light showed above the mountains.

There was something about being up and around, of going through the motions of making breakfast, that made his fear recede, made it seem puny. He cooked the last packet of cheese omelette, and it was when he was drinking the last of the tomato juice that the thought returned which comforted him more than any other: If the cougar had planned to attack, it would have done so yesterday when it had the chance—either when Doug was alone in the woods, or the minute they were in the clearing together. And Doug was an easy target. If the cat had not bothered him then, why would it do so later?

New thought: Maybe it hadn't attacked yet because it had just eaten. Maybe it would attack when its stomach wasn't so full.

Still, the way the cougar had behaved—darting from tree to tree, like it was playing hide-and-seek. No, Dad would say. The biggest mistake you can make is to believe wild animals think like humans. Lions don't think like humans; they think like animals. Doug's mind swung back and forth between fear and excitement.

But there was another picture forming in his head now. A picture of Doug going off to the high meadow, coming back as he had yesterday with the cougar doing a U-turn in front of him, and performing the whole bit in front of Gordon, who would probably be back by noon. Wouldn't that be something?

His temples pulsed with the thrill of it. If he were to walk calmly back into camp with a cougar beside him—well, not *beside* him, exactly—it would erase forever what had happened up on the ridge two summers ago. Gordon, who had once met a bear cub and almost freaked out. Oh, man, what Doug wouldn't do to just repeat what happened yesterday in front of his brother.

He waited another hour, going over the pros and cons and working up the courage, and then decided to try it again. Dad hadn't given them any precautions about what they should do if they *did* see the cougar. He assumed, Doug knew, that his sons would use the common sense he'd taught them when meeting up with any wild animal. Don't feed it; don't approach it; don't startle it—just give it room and quietly go on about your business. There were no warnings about cougars in the pamphlets they'd picked up on backcountry camping. This was obviously such a rare occurrence that no one thought to mention it.

Even as his head told him all the reasons he should not go, he stood up to leave. He would be cautious: Same pace, same clothes, everything the same as before so he would be completely familiar to the cougar, should it show itself again.

Next question: What should he take with him? Notebook in his pocket, camera over his shoulder, same as before, but keep his hands free.

With his heart pounding fiercely the minute he entered the woods, Doug made his way up the rocky hill to the meadow, alert to every sound, every movement in the underbrush. Each time he climbed up on a boulder, he expected to see the animal crouched there on the other side, and he found that he was more frightened when it was not in view than when it had been several yards off to his right. But the cat did not come.

He waited a long time on his observation rock in the meadow, but saw nothing, and was more disappointed still that the cat did not show up on his way back to camp.

Gordon was not there, so it was just as well. Because Doug would go back to the high meadow that evening—same time, same place—and *this* time, if the cougar followed him back, Gordie would be there.

He lay on his sleeping bag that afternoon and read one of Gordon's track magazines. He read more about shin splints, endurance training, and hamstring injuries than he really wanted to know, and finally decided it was mostly one big ad for running shoes. He tossed the magazine on the ground.

He had honestly expected that by late afternoon, dinnertime at least, Gordon would be back. Had even saved the Swedish meatball packet for him—sort of a peace offering. Boy, if Mom and Dad knew that Gordon had left while they were gone, and that Doug was here alone, they'd be mad. If the ranger came by and found out Gordon had gone off to the Comanche Peak Wilderness and left Doug alone, he'd be sure to tell Dad, and Gordon would really catch it.

Once or twice, Doug remembered, Gordon had stayed up on the mountain for two nights instead of one. Mom and Dad never worried, so okay, let him stay. He'd manage to get back just before the folks got here, and pretend he'd never left. Doug didn't care.

He ate dinner early, not because he was hungry this time, but because he wanted to get it over with and go to the meadow. Maybe the cougar came around only in early evening.

Again he tried to keep his pace measured, same walk, same step. He was not halfway through the woods before the cougar showed itself—darting from tree to tree.

Fear again. If Doug could cut it out with a knife, he would do it. Toss it away. Have done with the swell of dread that rose up deep in his chest, pushing rudely against his heart. If he couldn't control his fear any better than this, he might as well go back right now.

He decided he would go as far as the rock outcrop at the bend, and then see what he wanted to do. This time, he discovered, the cat made no semblance of hiding but loped along easily, staying almost even with Doug, or a little behind him, off in the bushes.

Doug would stay. Go the whole course. Excitement was nudging the fear inside him, making room. Again Doug decided not to stare directly into the cougar's eyes. Not yet. When he looked at the cat, if was a sideways glance, though he could sense the large animal checking him over from time to time. And again he felt a small measure of reassurance, especially when the cougar allowed itself to be seen. But then, strangely, it would slow down, so that it was lagging behind, making Doug drip with perspiration, before it came bounding silently through the trees once more.

When Doug reached the meadow, he thought he might have lost the cougar. The animal seemed to have disappeared entirely. What did he do now? When he had come before, he had sat on the rock for an hour. Who knows how long the cougar had been tracking him before that?

He decided to keep to the routine, and took his place on the rock, waiting. And then, as he looked, he saw the cougar come out of the trees twenty yards off, and simply lie down on the ground, head and torso upright, but legs sprawled out behind. Doug had to smile. For the first time, he could feel the fear melting away like wax.

The cougar always kept its head turned in another direction. Even when Doug changed position, its ears twitched at the sound, but still it fixed its gaze elsewhere.

Pictures. Doug needed pictures. He took a chance. He aimed the camera far up on the hill and clicked the shutter, a picture of nothing. He aimed it toward the side, and clicked it again. A picture of trees. And then, because the big cat seemed undisturbed, he slowly turned it in the direction of the cougar and clicked. The cat never stirred.

Wow! Wait till the guys see this one!

After a half hour, Doug rose slowly. Without even looking at him, the cougar rose, too, and ambled off into the trees. Doug could not see the cat as he started out, and once again, his fear made itself felt. But shortly the cougar appeared again, off to his left this time, and Doug could not help grinning as he started back.

If Gordie only knew!

Still, the closeness of the cougar and its tendency to trail, to let Doug move ahead a few feet, staying just out of his line of vision, brought a slight uneasiness. But Doug kept walking and, just as before, when he reached the clearing the cougar disappeared.

CHAPTER 9

DOUG SCARCELY THOUGHT ABOUT GORDON THAT NIGHT BECAUSE HIS mind was on the cougar. What it might be like, when the family was here, to walk out of the woods some evening, the cougar off to the side, and say, "Hi." See the expression on Gordie's face. Tomorrow they would all be back, and maybe it would happen.

From everything he could tell so far, the cat was merely curious, or perhaps it wanted company of sorts—the way it had waited for him while he was at the meadow, stretched out on the ground for some forty minutes, then ambled back when he started out again.

As he ate breakfast the next morning, Doug worried that the

cougar might leave before he could show it to Gordon and the folks. How could he make sure it stayed around?

He couldn't. Had to take his chances. Could not feed it, touch it—intrude any way on the privacy of the big cat. They had each tested the other out, and established a little trust. That was the most he could expect.

It was important for his record keeping to find out whether the cougar came at all in the mornings, or appeared only at dusk. He would not go off in the brush himself looking for it; not take a chance at catching it by surprise in its den. He would take the same path to the high meadow every morning to see if the cougar would ever meet him then. List the mammal species you identify, the manual said. Record their activities. He thought of how his notes would read: Mammal observed: cougar. Activities: following me.

First the walk through the forest. Doug didn't know flowers but he knew trees. Ponderosa pine and spruce. No cougar. No other animals either. When the cougar was around, there weren't any others. But when it *wasn't* around, there weren't any either. The forest knew the cougar was near, it seemed, and waited.

While Doug was on the rock, however, hidden by foliage, he saw a squirrel foraging beneath the branches of a Douglas fir, and cocked his camera. Suddenly, from out of nowhere, a marten sprang, pinning the squirrel to the ground and killing it with a bite to the base of the skull.

It happened too fast for Doug to get a picture. He didn't even try, he was so taken by the drama. Doug was so unnerved by what had happened, in fact, that even when the brown marten stood erect, triumphant, the squirrel dangling limply from its jaws, Doug forgot to press the shutter. A battle of life or death was over in seconds, and all Doug could think of was that the squirrel never had a chance. It shouldn't have turned its back. The thought came to him again: It shouldn't have turned its back.

He stayed on the rock long enough to get a picture of a couple of marmots courting, giving off their strange whistles and screams, their "tooth chatterings" when they detected danger. And just as he prepared to leave, he saw a pika pause at the top of a boulder. With scarcely time to snap the shutter, Doug wasn't sure he got more than its hind feet as it dived over the other side.

It was an exceptionally gorgeous day, and the only reason Doug thought about it—he usually simply accepted a beautiful day as the way it was supposed to be—was that Mom would have remarked about it. If she had come up to the high meadow with him in full sun, she would have pointed out the white and yellow and lavender flowers and named each one. Exclaimed over the red flower that looked like a tiny pineapple. The only wildflower Doug recognized on his own was the blue columbine, and that was because it was Colorado's state flower. He'd seen it in a book.

He spent the afternoon waiting for evening. Gordie should be back any minute. Boy, he was really asking for it if he wasn't here when the folks got in. Clouds gathered over the far mountain but dissipated without bringing rain. He fought off the temptation to go to the meadow early. It seemed important he keep to the schedule until . . . until what? Until he was absolutely sure of the cougar? Would he ever be? I watch its eyes . . . , the woman had said. It was the one thing that kept coming to mind.

As pleased as he had thought he would be at having the camp to himself, Doug discovered there wasn't much to do when no one else was around. It didn't take much time to wash his own dishes, tie up his own trash. He rarely changed his clothes. He even welcomed digging his latrine for giving him something to do. A heck of a lot of time each day must have gone into quarreling with Gordie, scuffling, arguing, because when Doug glanced at his watch, the hands seemed scarcely to have moved at all.

Around four, he decided to go to the stream and fill up all his empties. It would please Mom when she got back that evening. So he set off with a gallon-size and three half-gallon jugs in his hands.

He had not gone ten feet, was not even out of the clearing, when he saw the cougar standing at the head of the trail, its amber eyes fixed on Doug.

The momentary flash of fear gave way to pleasure. Wary still, but without even breaking stride, Doug said, "Hi, Charlie," then grinned. Like it was some guy from school. He wondered what the cougar would do when he headed down to the stream instead.

Out of the corner of his eye, he could see the large cat pause where he made the turn, then come galumping down behind him, heading for the stream below. This time, however, it fell in so close behind him that he could feel its breath on his skin as it investigated his ankles.

He could feel himself sweat. *Smell* himself sweat. The scene he had witnessed earlier between the marten and the squirrel came rushing to mind. It shouldn't have turned its back. But he kept his footsteps steady, his hands, holding the jugs, swinging along easily at his sides, and after a moment or two, the cougar went back into the brush.

Fear was his constant companion, it seemed, and Doug hated that this was so. He hated the way it surrounded him like a net.

He tried to tell himself that he was a lot braver in this situation than Gordon would be. *Knew* he was. His dad? Doug wasn't sure. Growing up, he'd had the feeling that Dad wasn't afraid of anything. He remembered one time, however, when they were driving home at night from a basketball game, and an oncoming car crossed over right into Dad's lane.

Dad had managed to swerve off onto the shoulder at the last minute before the other car weaved back again, but for a while Dad was too shaken up to drive.

"It's things like this, that you can't control . . . " was all he had said.

Well, Doug couldn't control the cougar, either. Not entirely. But he was convinced that the big cat took its cues from him. As long as he didn't do something stupid he was okay, but that was the scary part—not doing something that would alarm the cougar.

On the bank, he slowly set the jugs down. He smiled again as the cougar lay down on its side some yards off, while Doug went about the business of getting water. It was then Doug realized the cougar was female.

He did not turn his back on her, but he still felt vulnerable as he knelt on the stream bank, half-turned away, with nowhere to go should the animal spring. But as he filled one jug, then another, and the cougar watched disinterestedly, he told himself that this, if nothing else, should convince him of her intentions. Here he was, a perfect target. One lunge and he'd be on his back. One bite to the base of the skull and he'd lie still in the water. The big cat simply looked away, and didn't seem to care.

When the jugs were full, Doug sat down on the stump near

the bank's edge, and looked off somewhere beyond the cat's head. The cougar returned the favor. And there they sat, politely ignoring each other.

"You my pal, Charlie?" Doug said soothingly.

The cat's ears twitched, meaning she heard, but the sphinx face never moved.

"Actually," Doug went on, "I suppose I should call you Charlene or something, but somehow that doesn't do it."

The cougar tilted her head slightly and gave a long tongue-curled yawn. A sign of appeasement in animals, Doug had read.

He tipped his own head back and yawned as well. The cougar languidly groomed her paws.

What would *Mom* say if she saw him sitting here like this? Doug wondered. Why couldn't he imagine her being afraid? She had fears of a different kind, he decided. She worried more about relationships, maybe. Danger points between people.

"I'm not looking forward to this . . . ," she had said as she left for Lloyd's funeral. She didn't have to worry about talking to Lloyd anymore, so what did she mean? Maybe it wasn't Lloyd she had resented all these years so much as her father. The way he had pit them against each other, her and her brothers, then held her back. Maybe she was really afraid of going to Boston and facing *him*. Of what she might say if she weren't careful.

As Doug stood up to go home, the cougar merely turned her head in his direction, as though acknowledging his leaving, then turned away again.

"I like you, too, Charlie," Doug said. Follow me home, he begged silently. Stick around long enough for Gordie and the folks to see you.

But this time the big cat stayed put, and Doug went back by himself.

When he got over to the tents, Doug saw that they were just as he'd left them. No camping gear strewn about. No dusty canteen on the ground. He looked inside his tent. Gordie's spot was still empty. He wasn't too surprised that the folks weren't back. There could have been all kinds of problems with plane schedules. But knowing their parents might be here, Gordie should have come.

He sat down on his sleeping bag and stared at Gordon's space. So what was he worried about? For all he knew, Gordon had decided to stay up there until Friday, just to spite him. In fact, isn't that *exactly* what he might have planned to do? Tell the folks Doug was impossible to be with and so, to keep from fighting, he just checked out?

Gordon didn't have enough food, Doug thought. Well, maybe if he ate sparingly, he did. Sure, if you really put your mind to it, you could get by with the food Gordon had taken.

Doug got up and went about fixing his dinner. After the dehydrated mulligan stew, which was truly awful, he was down to soups and vegetables now. Consommé, he read on one packet. He wondered why anyone in the world would make a soup called consommé, which was simply brown water with no meat or vegetables at all. He was doing okay, though. There was still some asparagus soup, black bean soup, and a Bannock bread mix.

As he was rinsing his dishes, he wondered if Gordon had taken his canteen, too, or only the half-gallon jug of water. How many quarts of water were you supposed to drink a day? Two at least. Gordie must be out of water by now, and Doug felt strangely relieved. Gordon would be home tomorrow for sure. Doug wouldn't be surprised if he and the folks both got in about noon.

He walked to the meadow as soon as the meal was over. This time he was greeted by a low growl, a yowl, and then a purr. At the growl, Doug's knees almost gave way, but at his, "Hi, Charlie," the cougar set right off in the direction of the meadow and waited patiently for the hike back to camp.

"Goodnight, Charlie," Doug said on the return trip, when he reached the clearing. The cougar watched him as far as the tent, then disappeared into the near darkness.

CHAPTER 10

ONCE DOUG WOKE THINKING HE'D HEARD GORDON COME IN.

"I figured you'd be back," he said sleepily, watching as Gordon wearily took off his backpack, let it drop on the ground, and unrolled his sleeping bag.

Then Doug opened his eyes and saw only darkness. He reached over and turned on his flashlight. Gordie's space was empty. He lay back and drifted into the dream again. But when he woke the second time it was daylight. Gordon's space was still empty.

It was possible, of course, that Gordon had come back and gone into their parents' tent to sleep. Of course! He certainly wouldn't want to share a tent with Doug if he could help it, not after that last fight.

Doug got up and went over to the other tent. But it was just as his parents had left it—their sleeping bags, a shoe here, a T-shirt there, a pair of sunglasses and the cardboard box with all their data in it. Everything but Gordon. The quiet bothered him more than he'd thought. Well, the folks should be home by afternoon. Dad would know what to do.

He wondered if the cougar had started coming around for that very reason, that the camp was so quiet, and whether or not she would continue to come when the family returned. Doug didn't think he would be able to stand it if the cougar left before anyone else saw her. He had pictures, but pictures weren't the same. Gordon would say that Doug hadn't really been that close, it just looked that way, that the cougar must not have known he was there.

For the first time, however, the cougar showed herself in the morning. Doug was dumping his dishwater over by the trees, and before he could even turn around, something bumped against his legs, almost knocking him off balance. The cougar turned around in front of him, then came back, rubbing against his thigh in the other direction.

He was tempted to reach down and rub her behind the ears, but didn't. Somewhere along the way the cougar had experienced contact with humans. Doug was sure of it now. But he also knew that their coexistence depended on his staying somewhat aloof. No matter what had happened in her past, the cougar was no longer a cub.

"How you doin', Charlie?" he said, and limited himself to that.

He decided to go to the water hole, just to see what the cougar would do. Charlie came right along.

Each time this happened, each time he tried something new, Doug felt another rush of amazement. He shouldn't be surprised anymore, but he was. Surprised and disappointed that there was no one around to share it with. Hang around till noon, Charlie, he thought. Just stay till the others see you.

Down, down, they went through willow and aspen and blue spruce to the cottonwoods and alders that lined the stream. They passed the beaver lodge, which looked as still as a deserted house. Doug knew better, however. By now the yearlings would have been driven from the nest to find their own mates, build their own lodges, and the parents would have become parents still again. A new brood nestled somewhere beneath the sticks and mud.

The cougar knew, too. She stopped a moment on the bank, tail twitching, eyes on the beaver lodge. Then, convinced that this was no time to go hunting, or that the beavers were simply out of reach, the cat moved off again to Doug's left.

There were no other animals at the water hole, as Doug expected. When the cougar came to either meadow or stream, she had it all to herself. She walked to the edge of the water, making paw prints in the wet mud, and Doug sat down some yards off and watched her.

The cougar bent her head. She could only flick up a few drops of water at a time with her tongue. It seemed to take her seven or eight minutes to fill up, Doug decided. Something else to put in his notes.

Satisfied at last, the cougar sat down. She looked about her for a time, ears like radar, twitching this way and that, and finally lay down on her stomach, head and chest still upright, welcoming the sun.

Did he only imagine it, Doug wondered, or was the cougar's head slowly tipping back, the neck stretching out, becoming longer, eyes squinting? And then, deep within the big cat's chest, came a rumbling purr. Doug smiled broadly.

"You're a gorgeous beast, you know it, Charlie?" he said, and would have given everything he owned to have a picture of her at that moment.

But going back, his thoughts were on Gordon. Gordie would be there this time. *Had* to be there. A half gallon of water would not be enough no matter how he rationed it. Doug still remembered their climb up the mountain two years before, how Gordon had drunk a quart all by himself when they reached the place he camped. In fact, Gordon drank more water on their hikes than anyone else in the family.

"Where does it all go, Gordie?" Mom asked him once.

"I pee a lot," Gordon had told her, and laughed. They all laughed.

Doug wasn't laughing now.

His second idea was that Gordon had thrown out caution and was drinking stream water unboiled. But that wasn't likely either. He remembered once on a hike when the whole family got lost and had used up their water. As a last resort, they each drank a few swallows from a stream. All but Gordon, who held out till they were home again. Everyone had been sick later but Gordon.

Doug also remembered something his father once said—that the thing they had feared most in their flight from Cuba was whether they would run out of water before they reached the United States. They had not brought enough for the seven people on the raft, they realized, and this was foremost on their minds. Gordon would have remembered that, too.

As he neared the open space in the trees, he could see out over the adjoining field, the mountains beyond, and the high cliffs in the foreground. He quickened his pace as he came into the clearing—almost burst through the flaps of the tents, first his parents', then his own. No Gordon. No parents.

Doug crouched down, balancing on the balls of his feet, arms resting on his knees, breathing heavily. He now knew what it was to worry. Fear had taken on a new face. But then another thought crossed his mind. Of course! The water filter. Why hadn't he thought of that? Not wanting to carry any more than he had to, Gordon had probably taken the one half-gallon jug of water to see him through the climb, and then he would use the filter the rest of his stay.

Letting out his breath, his shoulders slumped in relief, Doug went back outside and opened the box of cooking utensils by the stove. He stared dully down at the water filter. There was only the one.

He sat on the log, looking out over the field that led to Comanche Peak Wilderness. He could feel his pulse racing, and this time it had nothing to do with the cougar. The cougar, in fact, was gone. Doug had been so intent on getting back to see whether or not Gordon had returned that he didn't even know when the big cat had left him, slipping away as she always did into the underbrush.

He tried to focus his thoughts on the cat. Any other time that would be the high point of his summer trip to the Rockies. But nothing worked. There was a new fear now.

The sky was threatening rain, which put off all decisions for the time being, so Doug made lunch. The last of the powdered pudding. The Swedish meatballs he'd been saving for his brother.

Through the early hours of the afternoon, he sat by the log, standing occasionally to see if Gordon was coming across the field, then watching the thunder clouds gathering overhead. By two-thirty, the sky darkened. Lightning flashed across the open sky, several streaks at once, all connected. Thunder sounded from behind the peaks in the distance. Then the rain.

It was not like thunderstorms back in Virginia, where you got a few good streaks and a couple of crashes. Here the lightning seemed to ignite the whole sky, and when thunder crashed, the boom reverberated from range to range. The mountain summits were hidden by clouds. Rain and hail came slashing down sideways, pelting down, driving Doug into the tent. And when at last it was over, the ground below was littered with marble-size balls of ice.

Doug went outside, picking up a large ball of hail and rolling it between the palms of his hands. If Mom and Dad were on their way here, they'd be soaked. He hoped Gordon wasn't trying to get back in this. That he would have waited until the storm was over, then started out. There was still time. If he started right now, he could be home before nightfall.

He watched until his vision blurred. The field, the sky, field, sky. . . . But three o'clock became four, then five, six, and seven.

Why was there no word from Mom and Dad? Don't worry if we're not back before noon on Friday, Dad had told him. Yet it was evening now, and no one had come, not even the ranger.

Doug went to the high meadow because he felt that as long

as he sat waiting for Gordon, his brother wouldn't come. Let him leave, however, and he'd return to find Gordie doing the waiting, Mom unpacking all the food she'd bought. That was probably it. She and Dad couldn't get the flight they'd wanted, got in late last night, shopped this morning, and hadn't even left Estes Park till afternoon.

Doug was surprised to see that there were still remnants of hail as he climbed—it was gritty now on the ground, like rock salt. Everything smelled new, refreshed, from the rain.

It wasn't until he was halfway up the rocks that he realized the cougar wasn't there.

"Charlie?" he called. "You around here somewhere?"

There were no sounds but birds and insects, no sense that he was being followed. He went to his observation post and sat for ten minutes, but he'd left his notebook and camera behind, so he gave up and headed home.

All the way back, he was thinking that perhaps he was worried for nothing. Gordie wasn't stupid. He knew he had to have water. He knew he had to save enough for the trip back. Doug bet that as soon as he came out of the trees, he'd see a wet pup tent draped over one of the logs—see Gordon's muddy hiking boots lying on the ground. See Mom and Dad, anyway, and then Gordon was someone else's worry.

But when he came into the clearing and looked, the tents were just as they'd been when he left, and Doug knew, even as his feet turned to ice, what it was he had to do.

HE SLEPT VERY LITTLE THAT NIGHT. WHEN HE DID, HE DREAMED ONCE again that Gordon had come back. The conversation was as real as if Gordie were there in the tent. In the dream, Doug kept telling himself, "I *know* this is really happening. I can quit worrying now." Except that, in the dream, when Gordie put down his backpack, then turned, Doug saw that his whole side had been ripped open—bone and muscle and fat exposed.

Doug bolted up and looked at his watch. 4:20. His pulse pounded in his ears. He would not go back to sleep.

Maybe what he should do was try to find the patrol cabin. See if the ranger was there. But no sooner had the thought entered his mind than he dismissed it. It would take as long, or longer, to find the patrol cabin as it would to get up to where Gordon had camped. And if he went all the way to the patrol cabin and the ranger was gone? The cabins were often vacant for days—weeks, even.

Doug had no taste for food, but decided to eat as heartily as he could, knowing what was ahead. He ate the last of the pancake mix and syrup. While he rinsed his dishes, he realized there was still the possibility Gordon would return that morning. Get there even before he left, though that was unlikely. Doug might, however, meet him coming down the mountain.

"Didn't have you worried, did I?" Gordon would ask.

And Doug would answer simply, "Yes, you did."

But now there was still another worry: What had happened to Mom and Dad? *Plane crash.* Every time the idea edged into consciousness, Doug gave his head a violent shake to ward it off. Auto accident on the way back from Denver? What if Dad straggled through the trees to tell him that Mom had been killed in a car crash, and then Doug had to tell him that something had happened to Gordon?

The out-of-control feeling again, one fear riding in on the back of another.

Stop it! he told himself sternly. Focus on *now*. What did he know for sure *now*? That Gordon was not back and his folks were delayed. Don't borrow trouble, Mom would have said.

He tried to think what he should take with him. Water. That he knew. Whatever he carried, however, would have to be in his fanny pack. He wanted both hands free before he got to . . . He refused to think about it.

Food. He rummaged through the near-empty bag of trail food, looking for anything at all that could be eaten uncooked. An apple and walnut coffee-cake mix. A half box of raisins. Dried peaches. Medicines?

Doug went to the box in his parents' tent and took out the small first aid kit that they carried sometimes on hikes—gauze bandages, hydrogen peroxide, scissors, aspirin. . . .

Compass. Definitely a compass, though Doug had no doubt he could find the rock face and the route Gordon used to go up it. The place was imprinted forever on his mind, so careful he was to avoid it.

Dressing carefully—denim shorts, T-shirt, heavy socks, hiking boots—he tied a light jacket and the fanny pack around his waist. And then, holding his fear at bay, he started off.

Doug had not even reached the field when he turned back. Going into his tent, he tore a sheet of paper from his notebook, and with his ballpoint pen wrote a note that he pinned to the flap of his parents' tent:

Mom and Dad:
Gordon left for Comanche Peak Wilderness on Tuesday and hasn't come back yet. I didn't get really worried until yesterday (Friday) when I realized he didn't have the water filter with him. I'm heading up to his camping place on the rock face about seven A.M.

Doug

There was something about leaving a note. . . . Doug swallowed and went outside. He hadn't said good-bye, though he wondered if he should. Hadn't said he loved them, though they knew he did. Felt that any kind of a good-bye would doom him before he started. He was going up the rock face, that was all, he told himself—would check on Gordie and come back down.

As he left the clearing and started across the lumpy field, over mossy slabs of rock, he tried to imagine what his parents would say if they knew he had waited until Saturday to check on his brother. He wasn't sure. If they had been here, would they have gone looking? He didn't know that either.

Boy, Gordon, if you're doing this on purpose just to get me up there . . . , Doug thought. Wouldn't it be just like him, though?

"Just wanted to see if you could do it." That's probably what Gordie would say.

He tries something like that, he'll have the fattest lip he's ever had in his life, Doug thought, warming to the imagined battle. If this is a bluff, I'll really pound him.

Next thought: Maybe Gordon hadn't gone up the mountain at all. Maybe he had just gone out with his compass, the way he'd said he was going to do, to see if he could find his way back again.

No, Doug told himself. He wouldn't have taken his sleeping bag or pup tent. Could he be staying at the patrol cabin? Not likely. If the ranger was there, he'd want to know why Doug wasn't with him. In any case, Gordon would have made sure he was back by Thursday.

The three-hour hike from camp to the base of the mountain seemed booby-trapped at every step—wobbly rocks, ankle-scraping boulders, roots, thistles. No two steps, it seemed, were on the same level, so that one of Doug's feet was always up, the other down. Grasshoppers and butterflies leaped and flew over the terrain, mocking him as he slogged along.

The narrow beds of dry brooklets were caked with mud, but one running creek must have crisscrossed Doug's path several times, and each time it was a matter of walking across its pebbled beaches or wading through its soggy swamps before Doug made the leap, at last, to the other side.

He stopped suddenly, for a figure was coming toward him across the field. The cougar.

"Been to her den, I'll bet," Doug said aloud. Somehow the sound of his own voice comforted him, as though someone else were there. He wasn't doing this alone. "There are probably some caves up there in Comanche where she's got her den. *That's* where she was last night."

"Hi, Charlie," he said.

The cougar came straight on, one foot in front of the other, eyes on Doug's face, and when she was within a few feet of him, Doug saw that there was blood on her jowls and paws.

Fear sliced through him, pumping up his heart, draining his mouth of saliva.

Gordie?

The big cat paused, too, looking him over.

Gordon, and now me, one of his selves was saying, and once again, his second self took over the controls. Talk to her, the other self said.

"How you doin', Charlie?" Doug said, his voice a high rasp.

He felt a bump against his thigh, and then he heard the purr. The cougar rubbed against his leg, turned around behind him and came back again, the purr rattling in her throat.

Was it Gordie? Was it possible he'd never even made it into

Comanche, that the cougar was feasting on him a little at a time?

Charlie simply sat down on her haunches and began to lick around her mouth, her long tongue curling around her muzzle, then searching out the blood between her claws.

Gordon's blood? The dream, Gordie with his side ripped open. If Doug had only gone up yesterday. . . . Each terrible thought gave birth to two more.

Doug's stomach lurched. Numbly he started walking again. The cougar walked, too. *Gordie!* That's all he could think.

He stopped again, a sickening thought overtaking him as he stared down at the blood on the cat's paws. There were dark hairs matted in it, caught between the claws.

No! Doug went on blindly, swallowing and swallowing. He had to find out . . .

He had not gone a hundred feet when he saw something else—a dark lump on the ground ahead. And then, coming closer, he found the gory remains of a marten. *Jungle justice.*

His shoulders went limp with relief. "Oh, man, Charlie," he said, smiling. "Oh, man!" He laughed aloud, a trickle of sweat dripping down his back.

The cougar got down on her belly and continued her lunch while Doug looked on, waiting for the pounding of his heart to subside.

If Gordon had made any kind of path the last few years he'd been coming into Comanche Peak Wilderness, it was overgrown with bitter brush and wax current. By ten o'clock that morning, however, Doug reached the rock face.

They always seemed closer than they were, those mountains. It was only now he realized how much more he had to go—a two-hour climb, at least. A point a hundred feet straight up might mean a thousand footsteps up, down, and around, to get there.

Wild thoughts still plagued him. Perhaps the cougar had already gotten to Gordie. Perhaps that's why she had shown so little interest in Doug as food. Maybe she had eaten her fill on Tuesday, and was now lunching on the small wild things she found in the field.

Doug looked up the rock face. "Gordie!" he yelled, just in case his brother was on the way down, and close enough to hear him.

Gor-die the echo rang. How small his voice seemed. There was, of course, no answer.

Doug took a short drink of water from his canteen, then rubbed his sweaty palms against his shorts, and began to climb.

CHAPTER 12

WHAT SURPRISED HIM THE MOST WAS THAT HE FELT BETTER. PARTLY because here, at least, the climb was not all vertical, and partly because the decision had been made. A lot of the tension, it seemed, had been caught up in the deciding. Should he try it this summer? Make an excuse? Would he *ever* try it again? Never? And each time Gordon asked the question, the fear went up a notch or two.

He controlled it now by not thinking about it—giving his full attention to where his feet went this very moment, not then; what his hands could grasp on to now, not later.

His thoughts tumbled here and there. His father had once said the same thing—about decisions. That the hardest part about leaving Cuba was the decision to do it. Doug had never really understood that until now.

He tried to imagine his dad at nine years old, about the age of Ronnie Beck, the kid on the plane. Imagined him setting out one night on an oil-drum raft with his father, two uncles, an aunt, and two cousins, using a toy compass to navigate. The year before, Dad's favorite cousin had tried what someone else had done—hidden in the wheel well of a jet airliner to Spain. Except that the first person made it; the cousin didn't; he had frozen to death during the transatlantic flight.

"And that's when we decided to leave," Doug's father had told him once. "If we had stayed behind and buckled under, it was as though Josepha's death hadn't meant a thing—hadn't given us the resolve to try."

"What if the seven of you had died at sea?" Doug had asked.

"But we didn't," was all his father had said.

They didn't, true, but when a tanker picked them up eleven days later off the coast of Texas, one of the uncles was dead. The others were taken to a hospital and treated for dehydration and exposure.

Doug continued the climb. Thinking about Dad made it easier. Whenever the path diminished temporarily to where he could see out over the edge, he would say to himself, Is this as bad as Cuba? and the answer, of course, was always, No. Thinking about Gordon, however, and what Doug might find when he reached his camp, made him feel worse.

What path there was led over scattered pitches of bedrock, across ramps of boggy tundra, then climbed some more, becoming a narrow, zigzagging passageway. Doug followed the steep-slanting boilerplate rock, ledged with wildflowers, catching glimpses now and then of a distant snowfield. At one point he could see a ridge far above where he could just make out an elk cow leading her calf.

At times the journey seemed futile, for Doug would climb, scrabbling and panting, up the rock face, around steep boulders, then make his way, feet sliding, down another gully, losing all the altitude he'd worked so hard to gain.

He was dismayed that he was thirsty again. At this rate, there would be little left for Gordie, so he took the cap off his canteen and drank only a swallow.

Every time he stopped, the fear inside him grew larger, however. At times it seemed to be the climb that frightened him most; other times it was worry about his brother. And then, as though that weren't worry enough, his parents. He plowed on, keeping his mind on other things, trying to remember the wildlife he'd seen so far. Elks—he could use those in his report; a snowshoe rabbit—he'd use that one, too. And a marten. He'd also seen two Steller's jays and a gray jay. Too bad he wasn't working on a merit badge in Bird Study while he was here.

Doug was nearing the first ridge. At nine thousand feet, he'd read, oxygen was about half of what it was at sea level. He had no idea how high he was. Stormy Peaks, to his left, was over twelve thousand feet. With each ascending step, the air seemed to change. A mountain has its own weather, Dad had told him. At high altitudes, a hiker could encounter sunshine, rain, sleet, ice pellets, wind, and snow, all in one afternoon, sometimes even in the space of an hour. The weather changed minute by minute, valley by valley, range by range.

It helped to keep his mind busy.

"This isn't so bad," he said aloud, wanting to hear a human voice, even his own. "You've climbed a lot worse than this."

Walking along the ridge crest, he followed a route through a long granite fin that stretched like a roofless tunnel before him. He remembered this tunnel from the first time he was up here, and was reassured he was on the right path. If only it went on like this all the way to where Gordon was camped, he'd have no problem. He had strength; stamina. A climb like this, no matter how rocky, he could do forever, as long as there were sides to enclose him.

When he came out again into open space, the winds buffeted him. A hawk he had startled from a nearby rock flew directly past, so close that Doug could hear the steady flap of its wings. He held tightly to a rock, not wanting to look down, but did. It didn't frighten him particularly, because there was plenty of room between him and the edge. Over the rocky hogbacks slabbed with quartz and sprinkled with muscovite, he could see a tongue of aspen crowding the narrow gorge below. It looked like the set for a model railroad.

It occurred to him that if he were more like the other members of his family, he would actually enjoy a hike like this. He would have set out that morning with a feeling of excitement. Then he thought of Gordon and how this wasn't the time for adventure. What would he find when he got up there? All the possibilities . . .

That was another word to remember, possibilities. Almost anything was possible, Mom had told him once. But not everything was probable. Which was more likely, that he'd find Gordon okay up there on the ridge, or that something awful had happened? That he'd find Gordon okay, he guessed.

Which was more likely, that he would get around the ledge just fine, or that his foot would slip and he'd fall six hundred feet to his death? He shakily sucked in his breath. That everyone else would be able to get around the ledge without trouble he had no doubt. That he, Doug Grillo, could do it, was a different story.

So he tried to think of the climb as something ordinary. When he stopped at the next level place on the trail, not even winded, he took time to look out between the trees. He could just make out Longs Peak from here—"old granitehead," they called it.

Weird, he was thinking now, that there were probably a hundred climbers on it right this minute, and Doug couldn't see any of them. Looking into the distance at Longs Peak, in the quiet of morning, it looked peaceful and unthreatening.

It didn't fool him for a minute. He knew the stories of the people who had died. He knew about the guy who . . . Doug pushed the thought out of his mind. Don't! he told himself as he set off again. Concentrate on rocks.

Okay. Rocks. Precambrian rock, his dad had told him. The rock that formed Longs Peak was here before there was anything else on the planet. Heat and pressure changed sediments to harder and harder rock, until sediments became schist and gneiss, quartz and feldspar. Mica. Layers of rock. Layers that had their beginnings in some huge disturbance inside the earth. He'd done a paper on it once for science.

Doug didn't know why, but he felt a vague sense of discomfort, like some unpleasant memory tapping at the side of his head. No, he thought fiercely. He was doing too well. No unpleasant thoughts now, thank you.

The muscles in Doug's legs carried him easily with each stride. He forced himself to think positively, concentrating on his strength. He didn't even bother to rest at the next place the ground leveled out, but moved on around the curve of the mountain, inching down steep, rocky troughs chiseled out by water, then making his way through a long maze of rocky outcrops.

Layers. It came back to him now. That was the word that seemed so unpleasant. Layers of rock, he'd been thinking, that had their beginnings in some huge . . . Layers of feelings, of grudges. Wasn't that how Mom had described it, with her and Uncle Lloyd? One thing piled on top of another, she had said. So many layers we never did get to the bottom of it.

Would Mom have climbed this mountain to rescue Lloyd? Well, Doug was doing it for Gordon, wasn't he? So no, what happened between her and Lloyd was not the same as him and Gordie at all. She was right.

There was a noise behind him and he stopped. It was like a rock falling, tumbling—rolling behind him down the trail, too far back for him to have caused it. He turned and waited, seeing nothing, hearing nothing more, then moved on again.

At this point there was a vertical face of rock on one side of him, boulders and scrub trees on the other. With each upward step he took, the small trees retreated from the landscape, but the wide expanse of boulders remained. He liked that—liked a wide span between him and the gorge below, a monstrous guardrail. If ever the demon that terrified him in high places convinced him to simply fling himself over the edge and get it over with, the boulders would be there to say no.

Suddenly he felt that familiar thump against his thigh.

"Man, Charlie!" he gasped, leaning against the rock wall. "You scared me half to death!"

The cougar came up around him, looked at Doug a moment, then moved on, checking once to see if he was coming.

"Hold your horses," he said, unsure of whether he wanted her with him or not.

Was it conceivable, he wondered, that the cougar had a den up here? That she spent most of the day among the rocks, coming home each morning, then going out to hunt around dusk?

That was another thing to think about now, one more thing to occupy his mind. But thinking about Charlie led to thinking about Gordon, and Doug decided it would have been better if the cat hadn't come.

The rocky path far up ahead suddenly fell into shadow, and Doug glanced at the sky. The clouds overhead were hard to read. Dark around the edges, with the sun gleaming behind them, and the wind trying to push them, unwanted, from this part of the sky.

The farther Doug climbed, the narrower the stretch of safety on his left. When he first started out, there was nothing at all but trees and meadow, then trees and rocks, then mostly boulders and a few scrubby trees. Each time he stepped, however, the span on his left grew smaller.

Now the low, twisted trees gave way to rock entirely, and the span had narrowed to the point that Doug could see the gorge below almost continuously. The hillside seemed to be receding, the edge coming closer to the trail. There were a few places,

Doug was sure, where, if he were to lie down crosswise on the path, his feet against the cliff, his arms stretched above his head, his fingers would touch the drop-off.

He tried to redirect his thoughts.

"How you doin' up there, Charlie?" he called shakily to the cougar, who seemed to be waiting for him at the next rise. The cat stretched out her head toward the sun and panted, the closest thing yet to a smile.

But there was a drumbeat starting now in Doug's chest; he could feel it. Seemed almost to hear it. Like a foghorn out over a bay; the far-off whistle of a train. . . .

He thought of various guys in his troop—how they would be enjoying the trail about now, exclaiming every time there was a new view of the canyon below. He tried to imagine himself in their bodies, becoming Frank Jameson, for example, or Teddy Heinz. They were always the first ones to the top of any climb.

But it didn't work. He *wasn't* Teddy or Frank, he was Doug Grillo, who had come up this way with his family two years ago and had not been able to make it back without help. Now he was Doug Grillo here alone.

About two hundred yards more, he guessed, and he'd be at the spot. Snow-splattered ridges gleamed in the distance. He felt he could remember every rock, every root of the ledge. Should he stop awhile and get his nerve up? Catch his breath?

He kept going, making his way around the next bend. The wind was soundless, sweeping the sun-filled sky. And suddenly, there it was, sooner than he had thought. The span of safey on his left gave way entirely, and he was face-to-face with the Fear Place.

Even the cougar stopped, lifted her head, and sniffed the air. She looked down over the edge, then back, as if to see if Doug were coming.

I can't! A swell of fear engulfed him, and for a moment the trees far below seemed to come up to meet him. Clinging tightly to a scrubby bush growing out of the face of the rock, Doug stared without blinking at the ledge stretching before him, even narrower than he remembered. Was this possible? Could it have eroded to twenty inches in places?

There was nothing separating him from the edge of the cliff and a plunge downward. There were even places that the ledge tipped slightly toward the yawning gap, places where loose rocks and stones lay ready to trip him, make him skid.

He could smell the difference in the air here above the canyon, sharp and moist. It beckoned him downward, and each breeze seemed to punch him in the stomach, shoot upward, socking him again beneath the chin.

Far below him, the rocky floor of the canyon waited. He could see the tops of the trees, a meandering stream, boulders. He wondered how long it would take his body to reach the bottom. How it would feel to . . . *no!*

Immobile, Doug swallowed and tried to get a grip on his fear. His mouth felt as though it were lined with dust. He attempted to measure the length of the ledge with his eyes—the length of the place where his heart stopped pumping and his legs wouldn't move. *That* place. About nine yards to the curve, and a few yards more after that, if he remembered right. It didn't seem so long when he thought about it, but looking out there now, it seemed impossible.

Maybe there were times it paid to be cautious. Maybe there were places that only fools would tread. Hadn't his mother said something like that once, or was it "Where angels fear to tread?" If there was such a place, this was it.

Would he ever make Eagle Scout if he couldn't try something like this? Would he even *live* to make Eagle Scout if he did? One slip of the foot and . . .

Stop it. His other self. As though he never took any other kinds of risks—riding his bike at top speed around corners, for example.

Look at the ledge, he told himself, and see if you could make it without falling off if it was drawn on the sidewalk with chalk.

Sure, no problem.

Could he do it if it were only half as wide, drawn with chalk on the sidewalk?

Of course. A fourth as wide, even. Give him a path on the sidewalk five inches wide, marked with chalk, and he could go for a mile, never stepping outside the boundaries once.

Okay, then. He had twenty inches, minimum. Do it, he told himself.

It was the cougar who showed him how.

The cat simply walked out on the ledge, hugging the side of the mountain, but not too closely. Not leaning inward, as Doug tended to do. As he followed, and as he thought about it, Doug realized that were his body at an angle and he slipped, his feet would be pointing toward the edge of the cliff. He needed to keep upright. He would remember that chalk line on the sidewalk.

It wasn't so bad at first. The ledge varied in width between three and three and a half feet.

Three feet is a yardstick, he told himself. Three feet is the width of a kitchen table, the width of a cot. Probably wider here than his sleeping bag. Yet he lay on top of it on hot summer nights and never rolled off, not even in his sleep. He could do this. Piece of cake. He swallowed.

Ahead, the cougar's left hind foot seemed to displace a small stone at the side of the path, and it rolled over the edge. Doug heard it hit a rock below, then another. The cougar glanced toward the gorge and kept going, ears up.

The path was narrowing now, and somewhere ahead was the curve where it was narrowest of all, where he couldn't see what he was getting to. Somewhere, right on the bend, was the place he had flattened himself against the rock. *I can't.* The words seemed to be building up already in his throat.

He felt the needle pricks in the palms of his hands again, and in the soles of his feet. Felt the tightening of his butt, the rigidity of his chest, as though, if he tensed himself enough, he might be too stiff or too hard or too impenetrable to topple.

Ahead, the cougar's body swayed with every motion, limbs sleek and relaxed. She took the curves as easily as a tire rolling along on its own momentum. She didn't walk carelessly, but in a deliberate, rhythmical manner, joints loose, paws secure.

As he approached the curve, Doug took a deep, shaky breath and let it out. Then another. He looked down at his feet and blew upward, to fan his face.

Jeez! His right bootlace was untied, the ends dangling.

He would not try to tie it here. Bend over here and he might lose his balance altogether. He would have to go around the bend dragging that lace.

Hollow-eyed with terror, his mouth dry, he began to maneuver himself around the narrow curve, watching each step to see where his foot would go next, scanning the wall of rock to see what his hand could clutch.

He would not allow himself to look down at the canyon. Would not let himself even glance at the large birds that were circling, soaring, just off in the huge space to his left. The cougar had gone on, probably so far ahead Doug would find it sitting beside Gordie's tent.

"Remember Dad on the raft," he said aloud, his voice trembling. He tried to remember the day Dad had told him about, when he was sure the sun would kill them all, broil them there in the open sea. They had seen a rowboat and paddled toward it, and when they got there it had four men in it, all refugees like themselves, and all of them dead. Was this as bad as that?

Then, answering his own question, he said aloud, "No."

He lied. It was worse.

He was still moving forward. Had decided not to face the wall and walk sideways for fear his repositioning himself might be more dangerous than walking straight. But just as he rounded the narrowest spot on the ledge, he came face-to-face with the cougar.

His strength almost gave way.

Was this it, then? He had come all this way to face a cougar who wanted to turn around and go back? Who would nudge him backward, step over step, possibly pushing between him and the cliff wall, sending him over the edge?

Their eyes were on each other—fixed solidly on each other for the first time. I watch its eyes to see if it's reverting to a wild state.

"Ch-Charlie," Doug said. "I can't get by. You've got to move."

The cat came on, so close her muzzle was almost against Doug's hipbone. Nudged him. And then the animal backed off. It seemed to Doug that her long body must be moving backward in sections, like a caterpillar. He couldn't see the rest of her, only that tawny head, the amber eyes, moving slowly away from him, leading still. She had not wanted to go back, perhaps; only wanted to see how Doug was doing.

Any minute Doug expected to hear the clawing, scratching sounds of a cougar falling over the edge. Things happened, even to the most expert of animals. And then Charlie disappeared silently from view. But when Doug took the last few steps along the ledge, he saw the cougar's tail ahead of him, Charlie having turned herself around again.

The path was widening here—on ahead, wider still. And finally there were scrub bushes to the left, making a safety rail between him and the canyon below.

He'd made it. Done it.

Charlie was sitting on the ground ahead, back legs down, chest erect. Doug crouched a few yards away, breathing heavily, his shirt soaked.

"Thanks, Charlie. Thanks, Charlie." Over and over he said it. She merely tolerated the nonsense, looking the other way.

He had made the ledge, but he was not home free. Fear of the Fear Place had given way now to fear of what he might see when he found Gordon. As he walked on, he realized, too, that he might have come all this way for nothing—that Gordon might have camped somewhere else. He also knew that, not knowing whether or not this was true, he'd had no choice but to come. The decision could only have been a yes.

The cougar had detected a camp, Doug was sure, because her nose seemed to be working hard, her head was up, ears alert. Over the rise were the stream and waterfall. Doug could hear the falls.

But when they came within sight of Gordon's camp, the cougar hung back. Doug saw the clump of trees, the pup tent beneath, a string hammock between two of them. As he drew closer he could see Gordie's hiking boots on the ground, a couple of food packets.

"Gordie?" Doug called.

No answer.

He came closer still, and then he saw the stockinged foot, unmoving, just inside the tent.

THIS TIME THE FEAR WAS DIFFERENT——NOT THE NEEDLE PRICKS IN THE palms, not the tensing, but a heavy, stomach-sinking kind of coldness that almost took his breath away.

Whatever happened to him up on the ledge was, in large part, up to him. What he found in the tent had already happened. Totally out of his control.

Doug got down on his hands and knees and crawled through the open flap.

Gordie appeared to be sleeping. He was on his back, his canteen open and empty beside his right hand. The place smelled of urine.

"Gordie?" Doug said again. He *looked* all right. No sign of an attack. Was he faking it? He shook his leg slightly.

A moan came from Gordon's lips. *"Don't!"* His arms flailed wildly as he opened his eyes and tried to sit up. And then Doug saw that his right foot lay at a sharp angle to his leg, and knew at once that a bone was broken. Gordon seemed confused, and stared at Doug, disbelieving.

"Gordon, it's me. What happened?"

"Doug . . . !" Gordon's lips were pale and parched, dried saliva in the corners.

Doug immediately unscrewed his canteen and held it to Gordon's lips. At first Gordon didn't seem to realize what was happening. Water spilled out the sides of his mouth. Then he clutched one hand over Doug's on the canteen and tightened his hold. *Glug, glug, glug . . .*

"Easy," said Doug.

The hand pressed harder, and Gordon went on drinking, drinking.

"Easy!" Doug said again, trying to pull it away. "Gordon, this is all I've got for both of us. It's got to get us back down again."

He tried to yank it away. Gordon hit at him, and Doug let him have a few more swallows before he got it back and put the lid on. It was half gone. Why the heck hadn't he brought the water filter, at least? Dumb, dumb, dumb!

"What happened?" Doug asked again.

"I broke my ankle. My leg or my ankle. Tell Dad . . . to take a look at it."

"He's not here. The folks haven't come back yet."

"Then how . . . ?" Gordon seemed disoriented. He rubbed his eyes.

"I came up because I was worried."

Gordon licked his lips. "Give me more water, Doug. I'm so *thirsty. . . .*"

Doug unscrewed the lid again and took a small drink himself. Could he get down the mountain on that? Another small swallow, then he held the canteen for Gordon and let him finish the rest.

"How did you get up here?" Gordon wanted to know. His eyes didn't look right. I watch his eyes. . . . Any other time the thought would have been funny.

"Climbed. How'd you break your leg?"

"The rocks. By the falls. Slipped . . ."

"When did you fall?"

"I don't know. What day is it?"

"Saturday."

"*Saturday?* Uh . . ." Gordon lay back with one arm over his eyes.

Doug gently shook his arm. "Gordie, when did you fall? It's important."

"Yesterday, I guess. No, maybe the day before. Wednesday? I don't know. . . . I dragged myself in here and haven't been out of the tent."

"Let me see your leg."

"Don't!" Gordon pushed himself up and gave Doug a shove.

"I've got to see it, Gordon. I'll have to put on a splint."

Doug was surprised to see tears behind Gordon's eyelashes. His brother lay down again.

Doug carefully pushed up the leg of Gordon's jeans and tried not to register shock. It was a wound right out of his Scout manual. Not only did Gordon's foot seem to be pointing in the wrong direction, but there was an open wound above his ankle.

Splintered pieces of bone were sticking through, matted with blood.

"How bad is it?" asked Gordon.

"Compound fracture." Be calm and cheerful, the manual had said. "We'll get you to the hospital; they'll fix you up."

He'd had the idea, coming up, that if Gordon was hurt, he'd take care of his immediate needs and wait with him until the folks came. Now he knew he couldn't wait, because he didn't know what had happened to his parents. Even if they made it back by evening, they wouldn't climb up here in the dark; they weren't crazy. So tomorrow would be the soonest they could get here. What if it rained tomorrow—if there was a storm, and they couldn't come even then?

He sat back on his heels and tried to think. If Gordon had broken his leg Wednesday or Thursday and was still conscious, then he probably wasn't in danger of shock, and certainly not of bleeding to death. What about earthquake victims? Soldiers hurt in battle? Didn't they get bones set days after they were hurt sometimes? Better to wait and do it right, than try to move Gordie and make it worse.

"What are we going to do?" Gordon's voice.

"I don't know. Let me see that wound again." Doug took out his knife and cut the cloth in the jeans so that Gordon's leg was exposed up to the knee. The skin around the wound was fiery red, swollen and hot. He couldn't take chances. "I'm going to take you down," he said abruptly.

"When'll they be here, do you think?" Gordon asked.

"We're not waiting for them, Gordon. We're going now."

Gordon rose up on his elbows. "How?"

"Your route."

"The ledge?"

"Yeah. I made it, didn't I?"

"I can't put any weight on my leg, Doug!"

"I'm taking you down piggyback."

"You're nuts!"

"Not any crazier than you, coming up here with the folks away."

Doug opened the first aid kit, but found little he could use. Uncapping the bottle of peroxide, he gently poured the whole thing on Gordon's wound, not knowing if it would help or not. The liquid bubbled up into yellow foam, fizzing slightly.

And then Gordon yelled.

"That can't hurt much, Gordon. It's only peroxide."

Gordon's eyes were huge.

"Gordie, I'm not even touching you!" Doug declared.

Inching backward on his hands and bottom, Gordon pointed desperately toward the opening of the tent. Doug turned, then grinned.

"Relax," he said. "It's only Charlie."

Doug told about the cougar in chapters, while Gordon ate the food he had brought—ate the coffee-cake mix with his fingers, unbaked. Doug made a story of the cougar. First chapter: When Charlie Came. And all the while, he was taking the tent apart, wrestling the aluminum poles from the fabric to use for the splint. Second chapter: The First Time Charlie Sniffed My Ankles.

"You have to pee, Gordie?" he asked when the food was gone.

His brother looked embarrassed. "I can't get up. I've just been rolling over on my side and doing it."

"Well, roll over again. You want to go before we start back."
Gordon slowly turned, wincing. "You don't have to watch."

Doug went off to the bushes himself, then over to the waterfall.
He wondered if anyone else had ever been up here. Probably. If
not, it really should be named for Gordon. Gordon Falls. It seemed
to lack a little something. Grillo Falls. He liked that better.

The pool beneath was not deep. Doug took off his socks and
hiking boots and waded in up to his knees, just to cool his feet.
He could feel the smooth surge holes in the granite. Around the
pool, the rocks were damp and mossy. He filled his canteen from
the falls, knowing that even this water was better than no water
at all.

There was movement off to his right, and Doug looked up.
Charlie had lowered herself almost flat to the ground. Her
haunches were bunched up, tail quivering, and with lightning
speed, she charged. There was a high-pitched squeal some distance
away, and Doug could just make out a pika, limp in her paws.

"Oh, man!" came Gordon's voice from the opening of the tent.

Charlie rested a moment, sniffed her catch, and then started
eating.

Gordon said nothing, only stared.

With his hiking boots on again, Doug set to work making
fabric strips from one leg of Gordon's jeans, which he had cut
off all the way around. He made cuts at the edge of the denim,
then ripped each strip down and off. Another and another. He
wrapped one of the tent poles around and around with his
windbreaker for padding, then used Gordon's windbreaker for
another, and bound the poles to Gordon's leg with denim strips.

"You sure this is really happening?" Gordon said, continuing
to stare at Charlie, who sat off by herself, licking her chops

contentedly. "I've had some strange dreams since I fell, but they were so real."

"It's happening," Doug told him.

"How are we going to get all my stuff back?"

"We're not. I've filled the canteen, and that's all I'm taking. The canteen and you."

Gordon took a deep breath, held it, then let it out. "I don't think we should try this, Doug. You freaked out once, remember."

"We'll make it."

"I don't know. . . ."

"Well, I do. We've got to get you down. Listen, now. I'm going to carry you as far as the ledge, then rest. We'll do the ledge, and then a piece at a time from there." He wished he felt as confident as he sounded.

You do what you have to do: Philosopher Ronnie Beck.

The hardest part was getting Gordon up on Doug's back. The only way Doug could manage was to squat down and then struggle to his feet, carrying Gordon.

"Oh, man, it hurts!" Gordon said, sucking in his breath each time Doug jostled him. His right leg stuck out at a strange angle once the splint was on, and Doug was thankful it had not been his left. This way the leg stuck out into space instead of bumping against the rocky face of the mountain and possibly sending them over.

Once Gordon was on, however, Doug grasped his brother's thighs and shifted Gordon's weight a few times to see where it felt most comfortable—moved the canteen so it wasn't in the way. Could he do this? Even twenty pounds lighter than Doug, Gordon was heavier than he'd expected.

"Ready," Doug said aloud, wanting to hear it, wanting *someone* to say it. "I'll need my left hand free, so you'll have to keep that leg wrapped tightly around me."

The cougar was ready, too. The pika had been merely an afternoon snack, and Charlie was already waiting at the edge of the cliff, sniffing the air. Doug took a shaky breath.

Up until now, the activity and the talk had occupied him. He had been too busy worrying about Gordon to think about anything other than the problems at hand. But as he approached the edge of the ridge again, fear rose up in his throat like vomit, and he wondered if this was a terrible mistake.

CHAPTER 15

SO WHAT IF HE AND GORDON GOT TO CAMP IN ONE PIECE? DOUG WAS thinking. If the folks weren't there, what good would it do? With Gordon on his back, the going would be slow. It would be six o'clock at least before they reached camp, and he couldn't start out for the trailhead for help until Sunday anyway. It had to be daylight.

If he just waited here on the mountain until Mom and Dad made the climb tomorrow and took Gordon down, it would probably be Sunday evening, at the latest, when Gordon saw a doctor. So what difference did it make? Why risk both their lives trying to get down today?

"You don't think we ought to try it, do you?"

Doug realized that he had stopped some distance back from the ledge. The voice didn't sound like Gordon's at all. Sounded like it belonged to some little kid.

"I'm thinking," was all Doug said.

Okay, if they stayed here, then what? They were out of water, but could get by on water from the stream. Giardiasis was really miserable, but it wasn't fatal. Then he thought of the wound— the redness and swelling. Remembered from his first aid book that if a wound gets infected, it could lead to blood poisoning. "If blood poisoning is not treated properly," his manual said, "death could occur in two days." What if Mom and Dad still weren't back? A lump rose in his throat. What if something had happened and they weren't coming back at all? And what if nobody knew he and Gordon were up here? By the time a ranger came looking, it could be too late.

"I think we ought to go," he said. He adjusted Gordon's weight one more time, despite his brother's groans. "You're going to have to stay really still now. Don't move around, okay? Keep your left knee tucked in as close to me as you can."

"Okay." Now it was Gordon's voice that sounded shaky. Wouldn't it be ironic, Doug thought, if he got himself up here safely, but died trying to get Gordon home? The first year they'd been to the Rockies, they'd heard a story of a seven-day search for a hiker who set out one morning for Pendleton Peak and was never seen again. Two men from the Civil Air Patrol crashed in a single-engine Cessna looking for him, and other searchers were injured, yet the hiker's body was never found.

If he and Gordon were to plunge off the edge of the cliff, would their bodies . . . ?

"No!" he said aloud. *Stop it!* he told himself.

"What?" asked Gordon.

"Talking to myself," Doug said, his mouth like cotton. "I'm going out there now, Gordie. Don't hold me so tight around the neck; I can't breathe."

"O-Okay." Gordon himself was breathing fast. Where his hands clutched Doug's shirt, Doug could feel their warmth and perspiration. And then, a moment later, Gordon's voice again: "Oh man, Doug, I don't know. . . ."

"We're going to do okay," Doug told him. He wasn't sure if it was bad or good that the narrowest section came first this time. After that things would be easier, but there was no practice, no time to get himself psyched. He knew he could get around the curve by himself now, knew what to expect on the other side, but could he do it with Gordon on his back? He took the first step.

"Get closer! Get closer! You're out too far!" Gordon bleated.

Doug took another two steps. "I've got to allow room for your knee, Gordie, now shut up. Stay as still as you can."

He could feel his brother's breath on the back of his neck. Hear it, for it came out in short, shaky gasps.

"The narrowest part is at least two feet, Gordie. We've got room."

"Y-Yeah."

Another two steps. Easy does it. Then another. They had gone two yards now. Ahead, the cougar walked confidently, torso swinging, limbs loose, checking out the sky. She stopped once and looked out at the view, then ambled on, placing each foot down deliberately, staying in the very middle of the ledge. Doug mimicked her gait.

Some day, he thought, I'll do that. I'll stop right up here on the ledge and look around. But not today.

Heart beating double-time. Hand sweaty around Gordon's right leg. Sweat running down the sides of his face. His left hand groped for whatever he could find to hold on to. Doug wondered if he dared try to talk.

"Remember Dad . . . on the raft?" he said.

"Yeah?" Gordon's voice was no more than a whisper.

"The sharks? Storms?"

"Y-Yeah."

"This isn't as bad as that."

Gordon didn't answer.

Better not to talk. Doug needed his full concentration. He had gone about three yards now. Don't look down. Another step.

"We're over the worst," he said aloud. He balanced his load and took another cautious step.

With the next step, however, he heard a strange and sudden sound. The only thing he could think of was a giant humming-bird—sort of a whir.

"What's that?" came Gordon's voice.

And then they knew. He could feel Gordon instinctively lean in against the cliff, and Doug hugged it, too, as close as he dared. Rocks. A rock slide, tumbling end-over-end, plummeting down to the canyon six hundred feet below.

"Doug . . . !"

The rocks seemed to be flashing by in front of Doug, yet slow enough in their tumble that he could tell they were fist-sized. Why hadn't the Grillos used helmets when they climbed? Twice dumb! Dad never mentioned them. Well, he didn't know every-thing, either.

"Oh, god, Doug!"

But the barrage seemed to be ahead of them, and finally, a few rocks later, it stopped.

"Man!" Gordon's body was steaming. Doug could feel it go limp as he let out his breath.

"I know." Doug's own legs were so sweaty that the inner sides of his denim shorts were wet. He was thinking of the ledge again, of the loose rocks. Of the possibility that the rock slide had only begun. "I'll go slow," he added.

What if they got around the curve to find it blocked? Where was Charlie? What if she'd been hit, and her body was blocking the way?

It seemed to Doug as though he were barely moving. I've gone four yards now, he told himself. Left over right, just like the cougar. Nice and easy. . . .

"The path is widening to three feet here, Gordie. Three feet is a whole lot. . . ." They'd come five yards. Almost halfway, perhaps.

He started to move forward, but was suddenly, unaccountably, yanked back again. What . . . ?

For a split second, Doug felt he was losing his balance, but regained it and stood trembling, heartbeat crashing against his ribs.

"What happened?"

"I . . . just had hold of a root," said Gordon.

"You idiot! *Don't!* Don't hold on to anything. You want to kill us both? I almost lost my balance!"

"Okay . . ."

"I *told* you to keep still, not to do anything." Doug was seething as he moved slowly forward again. To come all this way to risk his life for Gordie, and then have Gordon do something dumb like that. Easy, he told himself. Three more yards to go. Don't lose your cool.

It's three and a half feet wide here, Doug thought, and would be wider now with each step he took. Three and a half feet seemed an incredible measure of safety now that the two-foot mark was passed. Charlie stood at the end of the ledge, waiting. She was safe.

One more yard. Two more steps. And then the ledge was behind them, as rocks appeared on Doug's right. He kept going until he saw a large boulder on his left, then eased Gordon down on it, wordlessly uncapped the canteen, and took a long drink.

They passed the canteen back and forth, their breathing heavy. Gordon kept wiping his forehead, whether because of the ledge or the pain, Doug wasn't sure.

"Oh, man," Gordon said, half closing his eyes.

Doug couldn't say anything for a while. Tried to make his head go blank so that his heart would stop racing. Gradually he could feel his pulse subside.

The cougar came slowly up to the rock where they were sitting and sniffed at Gordon.

Gordon jerked backward, wincing.

"Just checking you out," Doug said. "Sit still."

But there was something about the cougar that seemed different this time—the tension in her flank, perhaps.

Blood.

Doug's body went cold. She smelled Gordon's blood? His wound? Did she see him as weak? As prey?

Gordon suddenly threw his hands up over his head, stretching his body up to its fullest, and yelled.

The cougar backed off.

"She smells my wound, Doug! Put me on your back! Let's go!"

Doug stared at the cougar. The amber eyes. She went on down the path a way and sat down.

"What good will that do, putting you on my back?" Doug asked numbly.

"Didn't you read that warning on the bulletin board at Park Headquarters?" asked Gordon.

"What warning?"

"About cougars coming down into Estes Park. I read it while Dad was picking up his permit. It said that mountain lions are intimidated by height. If you see one and you have a kid with you, you put him on your shoulders to make you seem taller. It said you should carry a big stick and make a lot of noise. Fight it off."

Doug's eyes were fixed on the animal. This wasn't the way it was supposed to be! How could they have come this far together, he and Charlie, only to end up enemies?

"She probably wouldn't have hurt you," he said, still disbelieving.

"Well, you don't know that for sure! You come up here with all those stories of a tame cougar . . ."

Doug felt his jaw tightening. "You have a problem with that?"

Gordon cast him a quick glance.

"Come on, get on," Doug said, turning so that Gordon could climb on again. He heard Gordon groan as he swung his bad leg forward and Doug grasped it.

There were still places they could fall—places where, if they stumbled and rolled a few feet, they'd go over the edge. But Doug wasn't afraid anymore. Too teed off at Gordon to be afraid, and for the first time, conscious of how tired he was. At the same time, he could not help but realize that everything he'd done so far toward the cougar had been wrong. He had *not* carried a stick, had *not* made noise, *not* tried to make himself look taller or to scare the lion off. But it had worked, hadn't it?

Here and there a shrub appeared, a bush, a scruffy tree, bare on the windward side. With every hundred feet, the trees on the right became thicker, until finally Doug got only an occasional glimpse of the canyon below. On up ahead, Charlie sauntered along as though the incident were already forgotten.

But tension and fatigue were beginning to have an effect. Doug was already exhausted from the climb, and now he had to retrace his steps with almost twice the weight. Three or four minutes was as long as he could go without a rest. Carrying a guy on his back while he horsed around at Scouts was one thing. Carrying somebody with a leg in a splint up and over logs and around rocks was something else. He stopped at the next large boulder and Gordon once again slid off onto his side.

"You're really pissed off, aren't you?" Gordon asked.

"What are you talking about?" Doug let out his breath.

"Just the way you're walking. Stomping down so hard. Every time you take a step, my leg feels like it's breaking all over again."

"Well, I'm still mad about what you did back there, but I'm not hurting you on purpose."

"All I did was grab hold of a root—in case you tripped or something, and you have a spaz."

"You would too if you were the one doing the carrying." Doug rubbed his own neck, massaging his shoulders. His arms were beginning to feel numb, his hands and fingers aching from the way they had clasped Gordon's thighs. He turned his back finally so Gordon could climb on. When Gordon made no move, he snapped, "Get *on*!"

Now there was an edge in Gordon's voice. "Look. Just go on without me."

Doug faced him. "Are you nuts? Get *on*!"

"Just forget it."

"Don't be a jerk, Gordie. You've been jerk enough already. Let's *go*!"

He was surprised to hear a tremor in his brother's voice. "*You* go on. Who needs you? You're mad about the cougar, too, and you know it! You know she was acting weird when she sniffed my leg."

"Don't be a *creep*, Gordon! I've had it up to here with you!" Doug was yelling now. Glaring. How was it he got stuck with Gordon for a brother? He'd take almost anybody else instead of this air bag.

But there weren't any other brothers. Gordon was it. For better or worse, Gordon was all he had. Whose fault was it they got along as badly as they did? Could they really say that Dad pitted them against each other the way Mom seemed to think Gramps had done with her and Lloyd? If the fights started with Doug and Gordon, couldn't they stop there as well? He'd saved Gordon's life, perhaps, by coming up here to get him, but was it possible Gordon had saved his? Theirs? By throwing up his arms and yelling—scaring Charlie off? No, Doug had *not* seen the bulletin on cougars.

"Look," he said finally. "Are we going to go the rest of our lives quarreling over dumb stuff?"

"Who says it's dumb? I'd rather crawl back than listen to you make like Mr. Big."

"Gordon, will you just shut up? For once will you listen to yourself, for Pete's sake?"

"Me? Look who's full of it!"

Doug wanted to cream him; knock him backward off the rock. Just pound and pound till he shut up. Instead, he turned away, just as he turned away from the cougar. When you're not quite sure what will happen, not quite trusting, Charlie had taught him, look away. The big cat was sitting on the trail doing it now—listening, but not looking.

Doug waited until he was sure he could speak without shouting. "You were right about the garbage on Tuesday," he said, forcing the words from his mouth.

"Yeah? Didn't I tell you?"

"Yes, you told me. I was acting stupid. And right now you're acting stupid. If I came up here like Mr. Big, it was all a put-on, because I was scared shitless."

Gordon gave a small surprised laugh. "Well, I was pretty scared myself."

"So for once we're even," Doug told him.

They sat silently for several moments.

"I just . . ." Doug stopped, wanting to rehearse it first in his head, then barreled on: "I just don't want us ending up like Mom and Uncle Lloyd."

There was quiet for a moment.

"I know," Gordon said at last. He took a breath and let it out. "Sometimes it . . ." He shrugged. "Sometimes . . . between us . . . it just seems to ignite all by itself, and I don't know how to stop it."

A trace of a smile stretched the corners of Doug's mouth. "Check out the eyes," he said.

"What?"

Doug grinned. "Watch the eyes and see if he's reverting to a wild state," he told his brother. "It's a story, Gordon. Get on and I'll tell it to you going down."

This is a day of firsts, he was thinking, as slowly, laboriously, he hoisted his brother on again. Sometimes the only person holding you back is yourself. He thought again of his mother. Why couldn't she have gone ahead and become a pilot anyway, no matter that Lloyd did it first? If she really wanted to do it, why didn't she?

That was a question he would probably never ask her, because the answer might be too painful to admit. Next thought: Maybe he would never ask it of Mom because he would never see her again. He pressed his lips together.

The sun broke through the cloud cover, but it was not a welcome sight. It made the trek more hot and tiring, the boys more thirsty. Sometimes it seemed to Doug he had to stop every two or three minutes, and each stop was an ordeal for Gordon. Once his brother cried out in such pain that Doug wondered if he shouldn't just leave him and go the rest of the way alone. But leave him with what? No food, no tent . . . and Charlie about? He knew as well as Gordon that it wouldn't be safe.

He talked on about the cougar, just to keep his mind off his own feet, his back. Wanted to make sure that all the good things were said before he and Charlie parted company forever. His tongue felt so thick and dry that he slurred his words, and wondered if he were making any sense at all. Sometimes Gordon responded, sometimes not. When he did, his breath was foul against Doug's neck—morning breath times ten. Once or twice his head fell on Doug's shoulder, then bobbed back up again.

It would take them twice as long to get back to camp, Doug realized now. Three times, maybe. Far too many stops. His legs might make it, but pain radiated all through his shoulders and down his back. He played a game of goals. With his eye on an object perhaps twenty or thirty feet ahead, he would tell himself that if he didn't make it to there without stopping, it was man overboard. Once there, he would set his sights on still another landmark—a tree, a log, a bush. . . . If he didn't make it to there without stopping, he and Gordon were shark bait.

It was not long however, before he knew he could not do this anymore. Gordon would have to walk. He slid his brother off the next time he found a high surface and, bracing one arm around Gordon's waist, Gordon's arm around his neck, they moved side by side, Gordon hopping on his left leg, trying to keep the injured one off the ground. But it was just too painful, and there were places it did not work at all. Too many rough patches that Gordon found impossible to maneuver. So Doug let him crawl onto his back again and they went a short distance more.

The goal was simply to get Gordon safely down the mountain, but there was an even longer hike to camp after that. And then what? What if he hiked alone all the way to the trailhead for help and no one was there? Up in this corner of the park, not too many took the trails.

Charlie was keeping her distance now, yet as long as the boys were moving, she seemed the same animal Doug had known before—the playful companion on their way to the high meadow.

Dissatisfied with Doug's slow pace, she'd lope on ahead, then circle back to see how he was doing. But Doug knew now what he'd tried to forget before: They were friends, but he was tame, and she was wild.

He continued to babble on for Gordie's sake, reciting everything he knew about cougars: "They're the same as pumas," he said. "Same as panthers." He jiggled Gordon slightly. "You awake?"

"Um . . ."

"What'd I just say?"

"Panthers . . ."

"You'd better stay awake, Gordie. I want you to be able to tell me how you feel. Okay? Gordie?"

"Uh . . . uh. . . . My leg hurts like crazy . . . throbs . . . What time is it?"

"Almost two. Stay awake, Gordie. Come on, now."

They had reached the base of the rock face, but it brought no joy. For the first time, Doug began to feel he truly might not make it. Several times he stumbled with weariness.

It was no use. His arms were giving out. . . . His back . . . But just when he decided that all he wanted to do was lie down, he didn't care what happened, he felt his other self taking over the controls—the guy in command. Just when that part of him that was still a four-year-old kid, crying that he couldn't make it, seemed to get the best of him, the older Doug would say, Come on, don't give up now. You've got him this far. You can do the rest. . . .

Once he lurched and, grabbing Gordie's legs tighter to keep him from falling off, hurt Gordon so that his brother yelped with pain.

"I can't do this, Doug . . . !" Gordon pleaded. "Oh . . . uh . . . oh man, it hurts so!"

Doug stopped, leaning against a rock, bending full forward to keep Gordon from rolling off.

"I can't leave you here, Gordie. How can I leave you?" His own voice sounded weird, his tongue swollen, it seemed. He pressed the side of his face against the rock, relishing the coolness against his temple, resisting the temptation to lick it with his tongue. He was so hot, so thirsty. . . . If the water they'd been drinking was going to make them sick, when would the symptoms begin?

He opened his eyes suddenly, then rose up just a little.

"Gordie!" he said. "Listen!"

Gordon was already edging off, slipping down onto the rock, then off into the grass.

Somewhat dizzily, Doug righted himself and listened again. There was the unmistakable sound of hoofbeats—the unsteady clop, clop, of a horse making its way across the rocky terrain.

"I hear it!" Gordon said.

Charlie heard it, too, for she slunk off into the bushes.

Doug stared hard into the distance. A man on horseback was meandering about, looking in first one direction with his binoculars, then another.

With every bit of strength left in him, Doug yelled. A pitiful sounding yell, more like a bleat. He tried again.

"Here! Over here! Hey!"

He waved. Gordon waved. And then Doug crumpled onto the ground beside his brother, as the man turned his horse in their direction.

He felt an arm around his neck, Gordon's head against his

shoulder, and then Gordon was crying, not making a sound. So was Doug.

As they watched the ranger coming toward them, Gordon said something that sounded like "please."

"What?" asked Doug.

"Pee-less," said Gordon. "I've been scared pee-less."

Doug laughed aloud. "Won't be anything left of us, will there, when we get back?"

The ranger brought his horse to a stop and dismounted, the binoculars swinging from a strap around his neck.

"Looks like you guys have some trouble here," he said, quickly coming over, looking down at Gordon's leg. "What happened?"

"He broke it," Doug said. His voice was dry and raspy.

"Are you Doug? The one who wrote the note?"

Doug nodded, almost too weary to speak. "How did you find it?"

"Saw it pinned to one of your tents," the ranger said. He was gently examining Gordon's leg, and gave a little whistle. "Headquarters got a call yesterday. Your parents got fogged in at Boston. Your dad wanted to know if we could get a message to you—tell you they'll be back in camp by tonight. . . ."

Wave after wave of happiness washed over Doug until he felt drenched in relief. He struggled to his feet, and helped the ranger gently lift Gordon, supporting his weight between them, then moved him around to the horse's side.

"I couldn't get over to see you guys right away because we had an injured hiker to take care of," the ranger explained. "I didn't know you were by yourselves, and wouldn't have put my okay on that, I can tell you. Seems your father left a note under the wiper of my pickup back at the trailhead, telling me you were by yourselves. What he didn't know is that I've been doing some work around the patrol cabin and didn't get out to the trailhead for several days."

Something else Dad hadn't thought of, Doug realized.

"Anyway, the call was relayed to me, and I figured to start out early this morning and look in on you with the news. That's when I found your note, Doug." He smiled just a little. "That was a good idea, except that Comanche Peak Wilderness is a heck of a big place. How in blazes I ever found you, I'm not sure."

Doug grinned sheepishly.

"Lunkenhead," Gordon managed to say, nudging him with his elbow.

Together the ranger and Doug hoisted Gordon up on the horse's back.

"How *did* you find the right place?" Doug asked, realizing how miraculous it was.

"I searched your tents, found the trail maps, and an old map with penciled markings of the Comanche area. Figured that had to be it. I've been riding around up here the last two hours, and was about to radio for a search. Happy endings, that's what I like. I'm also supposed to tell you that your folks' visit went fine."

Doug smiled some more. Mom had talked things out with her dad, then. Said some things that needed saying for years.

He realized that the ranger was studying him. "I'm going to radio for an ambulance to meet us at the trailhead, but how the heck did you get your brother down here?"

"His back," Gordon murmured. "He carried me down on his back."

"How long a climb up there?"

"Couple hours."

The ranger whistled again. "I think you both are going to need a ride back. Tell you what, let's see if . . ." He stopped suddenly, face frozen, then slowly reached out and took the horse's reins in his hand.

"Now I don't want you boys to panic or anything," he said, "but there's a cougar back there. We've had a couple sightings in our Front Range communities, but the cats don't often come around people up here. Looks to me like he followed you down the mountain. . . ."

Doug turned and managed a grin. "It's okay," he told the ranger. "He's a she, and her name's Charlie."